PANTS

by
WRJ Hyslop

ISBN: 978-0-244-64545-8

PublishNation
www.publishnation.co.uk

Chapter 1

Fanny and Bobby

"Next.".........

The girl in front of Fanny rushed in through the door to the vast auditorium of the Lyceum Theatre in London's West End. Fanny was next in the queue at the audition for the leading role in the latest big musical - The Sound of Music. She had never been this nervous before, even though this was her eleventh audition. The previous ten had all ended with the now familiar phrase "Thank you. Don't call us, we'll call you." She never liked to hear it but had come to expect it more and more, and even though she expected to hear it, it still hurt.

Ever since she was a little girl she had dreamed of being on the stage in fantastic west end musicals. She had dreamed of the fame, the glitz and glamour, her name in lights "Fanny Trump"..... Well yes.... She realised that it wasn't the best stage name but it was her real name and she just hadn't come up with anything better yet. Fanny just seemed to know that one day she would find what it was that she was looking for and she had a great feeling about this particular part. This one, she thought, was the one. The girl who had just gone inside the theatre began to sing and Fanny listened intently in the very unsporting hope that the girl was not that good a singer or, if she was a good singer that some inexplicable tragedy might befall her, like – she might fall down a hole in the stage or a big weight might fall on her head and render her incapable of singing and so Fanny would get the role of Maria the goatherd. "Wouldn't that be wonderful" she thought! Fanny was abruptly jolted back to reality when she felt a warm hand grasp hers followed by an arm round her waist and suddenly she was in a full on embrace with a long haired, bearded young man with black rimmed glasses wearing cricket whites who planted her with a big wet kiss, smack on the lips.

1

This was actually Bobby Blinkett, the love of her life, her childhood sweetheart and current boyfriend. Bobby and Fanny loved each other dearly and were together as much as they could be. Bobby always liked to be present at Fanny's auditions to offer her support ..... or rather to console her when she was given the rejection spiel.

Although Fanny was usually unsuccessful in her attempts to land a big part in these productions, she had many times landed smaller roles in less well known offerings.

For example, she had been chorus line in Seven Brides for Seven Sisters, a less well know version of the original of similar name but produced by the Lesbian and Feminist Musical Society. It wasn't that successful though and was pulled after a week of poor attendance and abysmal reviews. Another that they fielded was Olivia Twist, a feminist's view of the London pick-pocketing scene in the early 19th century, in which Fanny was cast as a rather grimy looking street urchin. This one actually ran for two weeks but they were closed down following a police raid and the producers arrested and charged for copyright infringement and gross plagiarism. The Lesbian and Feminist Musical Society was subsequently disbanded.

Fanny achieved a more reliable income performing in Pantomime, which generally ran from September to January, but again it was usually chorus or minor parts. It was however very valuable experience and provided her with a very welcome, albeit paltry, pay packet every week over the winter months. She knew she just needed to keep plugging away at the big stuff.

No sooner had Bobby arrived and planted her with the massive wet kiss than Fanny heard the call booming out "NEXT"..... Fanny felt her stomach do a triple back somersault and her heart leapt in to her mouth....figuratively of course.

"Goo on on gerl, knock 'em for six, I know you'll be great!" It was only now that Fanny was walking away from him, towards the theatre door, that Bobby could see that she was actually dressed as a little Austrian goat herd and he liked it. She was a naturally pretty girl Fanny and didn't need make-up, she had beautiful black hair neatly cut in a fashionable bob, usually, but today she was sporting sticky-out pigtails and a white milkmaid's cap and she had just the right amount of make-up. Bobby thought she looked gorgeous and so he followed up his words of support with a very loud wolf whistle which made everyone else in the queue look and made Fanny turn ever so slightly pink. The door to the hall was closed firmly behind her and Bobby remained outside but pushed his ear up to the door so he could hear what was going on inside.

"NEXT. Come on Miss, we don't have all day", said the very large casting director and as Fanny arrived at the spot. "Thank you. Name please."

"Fanny Trump", she said very meekly. (It was a little embarrassing).

"OK then Fanny Trump, let's see what you've got!"

The piano began to play and Fanny began to sing very sweetly and, it has to be said, very proficiently.

"High on a hill was a lonely goatherd
Lay ee odl lay ee odl lay hee ho-o-o ….."

Bobby had closed his eyes and was listening intently. Everything seemed be going great. Fanny was singing her little heart out, she wasn't putting a foot out of place. It really was a classy performance. Was this going to be the winning one? Was this going to be the one that catapulted her to fame and fortune? Bobby knew that Fanny had a great talent and that one day these people who sit in halls and theatres and choose the stars of the future would see this talent in Fanny, just as he did. Was it to be today? Alas, no, just as Fanny was taking breath to make a start on verse two the inevitable call was bellowed out from the second row back of the huge room where the casting director was sitting. "Yes, thank you. Miss Trump. Don't call us we'll call you…….NEXT!"

Fanny hung her head, turned away and made for the door. As the next hopeful pushed her way past Fanny to get to the spot Bobby could see that Fanny's eyes were filled with tears.

From inside they heard the casting director call out, "So you must be Miss Andrews" and the piano began to play and Miss Andrews began to belt out

"The Hills are alive with the sound of music."

3

As Fanny reached out to take Bobby's hand she shook her head and whimpered, "I think it's another 'No' Bobby".

"There, there my little precious bundle, you don't know that do ya? I heard you, singing like a bleedin' lark you was. It was beautiful my little cherry blossom. They must've loved it too….. and didn't they say they would call you?"

"Oh Bobby you are a bleedin' pillock sometimes." Bobby knew that they only said that and they never did call but it seemed to lift Fanny just a little. As they turned away to walk, hand in hand, out of the building with Julie bleedin' Andrews belting out more of that song Bobby turned to Fanny and said.

"That's just pants, that is!"

Chapter 2

Nappies

Fanny and Bobby's relationship went from strength to strength. Although Fanny was clearly focused on career she never forgot the lessons that her mother and father had taught her. Family was more important than anything else and she always had time for Bobby no matter how down she felt. Bobby always lifted her spirit and the disappointments didn't matter as long as she could be with Bobby.

Bobby too knew that he wanted to spend the rest of his life with Fanny. He loved her intensely but didn't like to be too obvious about it. That would not be cool. He was still a big kid at heart and liked to muck about with his friends. Having any kind of responsibility was the farthest thing from his mind but he loved to spend his time with Fanny and he yearned to be with her when they were apart. This is how he knew she was the one.

Fanny Trump and Bobby Blinkett were married on the 24th of September 1972. It was quite a zany affair. Fanny was dressed as Goldilocks and her three bridesmaids were all in bear suits. Bobby was very elaborately dressed as a very dashing fairy tale Prince. All guests were asked to attend in fancy dress - and they all did. It really was the most bizarre sight. The Mother-of-the-Bride was dressed as Old Mother Hubbard and the Father-of-the-Bride had come as Frankenstein's Monster. Bobby's brothers, Fred and George, were dressed as Tweedle Dum and Tweedle Dee and when Bobby's old Uncle Cecil turned up in a really excellent Mad Hatter outfit Fanny had a fit of the giggles because Bobby had always maintained that old Uncle Cecil was 'a few sandwiches short of a picnic'. The Vicar had had to steal himself a couple of times during the ceremony, not least whilst peering between the happy couple at the altar and he caught sight of some of the assembled congregations choice of attire and he felt a pang of remorse and cast his gaze skyward as if seeking forgiveness from the almighty for allowing the Devil himself to take a pew in row 12 between Marilyn Monroe and President Lincoln.

As Fanny had walked down the aisle on the arm of Frankenstein's monster and she beamed back at all her friends and relatives who had turned to watch her make her walk down the aisle she nodded her helloes and even waved excitedly to some. She had just caught sight of an unfamiliar yet strangely familiar face. A very beautiful lady dressed as a Fairy Godmother with snow white wings and a wand with a sparkly star shape on the end and a tiara and a beautiful pom-pom like tutu positively glowed with an almost electric, ethereal, pulsating glow and beamed a massive smile towards Fanny. Now who was that? Fanny thought. She could not work out in her head where or when she had seen her before and thought that perhaps it may have been one of Bobby's little known glamorous cousins she had fleetingly met in the past. She was past her very quickly and in all the excitement she forgot to look again. She never did see her again that day and Fanny thought no more on the matter.

Anyway, it was a wonderful day which went off without a hitch, everyone enjoyed themselves wholeheartedly and agreed that it was the most memorable way to celebrate ones marriage and the most fun that any of them had had at any wedding.

Bobby had lined up a new job and was due to start first thing on Monday morning, so, no honeymoon for poor old Fanny. Perhaps, they thought, they might get away somewhere after Bobby had settled in at work. Bobby's new job was in the printing factory a short bus ride from their house. He was to start in the packing and despatch section but he hoped to work his way up to the 'Humour' department writing new jokes for Birthday cards. It sounded like his dream job.

It wasn't long before Fanny was expecting a baby...... in fact, jump forward 5 years to 1977....and there are two toddlers playing with lego on the floor of a very chaotic kitchen of Fanny and Bobby's 2-up-2-down in Bexleyheath, a third, younger child is being fed in the high chair....or more accurately, is squishing pureed apple through her hair! Fanny was dressed as Tinkerbelle having just returned from an audition for a part in Peter Pan. She was almost certain that, again, she had failed to get the part and was feeling a little blue but managing to keep it together by keeping herself busy tending to the kids lunch. Her mum had offered to come over and look after the kids for the morning while, Fanny was at her audition, as she always did. She loved to babysit whenever she got the chance and it was usually for one of Fanny's auditions.

Bobby and Fanny's first child had come exactly nine months after the wedding, was a girl and they called her Zoey – Zoey Blinkett. Baby number two followed soon after (as soon after as it was medically possible), was a boy and was named Michael – Mickey Blinkett. The third, who by now was wearing all of the pureed apple on her head, was now almost a year old and was named Tallulah – Tallulah Blinkett. Fanny was a very busy mum these days with three very young, very loud, very demanding children AND she had to look after Bobby too. Bobby worked very hard at the factory and was usually very tired when he got home at night but always had enough left in the tank to enjoy a little play with the three children. On this particular Friday in June Bobby had managed to blag an early trap and so mid afternoon he came bounding in to the kitchen in his working trousers, cricket sweater and a sombrero.

"Hello my little darlin' angel, ha did it go?" Bobby was in fact referring to her audition. He hadn't managed to make it today as he had had other business to attend to. He had left work early in order to go and collect his 'big surprise' for Fanny and it was waiting outside.

Fanny began to tell Bobby all about the audition and became a little emotional and upset that, yet again, her hopes had been dashed. Bobby did his usual 'Chin up' routine and 'There's always next time' speech which Fanny had become accustomed to.

"Never you mind my little Cream Puff. I've got a surprise for you. Close your eyes and come aaatside."

Fanny did as she was told. Bobby held her hand and led her toward the door which he held open for her. When she reached the step she opened her eyes and found herself studying a rather ropey looking VW camper van. It was mostly yellow with a white roof and had a pretty flower-power design all up the side and a CND sign painted near the back.

"Well, what d'ya fink my little Sugar Plum? Isn't she a beauty?" said Bobby beaming with pride.

"It's lovely Bobby. But why?" said Fanny looking a little taken aback.

"We're all going on a summer holiday," sang Bobby. "But fink of it as a belated honeymoon my little honey pie".

"Oooh! That sounds lovely Bobby. Where will we go?" asked Fanny.

Bobby pulled a rolled up magazine from his pocket. It was an old National Geographic. He opened up the magazine at the centre pages which had a very impressive picture of some hairy cows at a lake with big hills in the background.

"SCOTLAND", said Bobby.

"Oooh! Very nice. That sounds lovely Dear!" Fanny paused and looked back to Bobby and turned side on to him rubbing both her hands over a very obvious pregnancy bump and said, "Oh and by the way my darlin', I'm pregnant."

Bobby looked first to her face and then to her bump and back to her face. He could not hide his surprise nor eventually his glee. "Well that's bleeding wonderful", he said as he pulled her in for a kiss and a cuddle. "The van's got 6 seats."

Chapter 3

Tartan Trews

The camper van, which was now noisily trundling along the M6 towards Scotland with Bobby at the wheel, Fanny beside him and the three kids strapped in behind, was a bit rough round the edges. It had certainly been well used in its lifetime and had a few bumps, bashes and dodgy repair jobs to show for it. Bobby reckoned it was only on its second time round the clock but Fanny thought this unlikely and wouldn't be surprised if it was four or five times round the clock and of course this would mean that the little van had been to the moon and back (in mileage terms). The kids, obviously, got the wrong end of the stick and thought that the camper van had actually been to the moon and back and wondered if they could possibly take a detour to take in the moon on the way to Scotland. They were also very impressed that their Daddy had had the foresight to buy a camper van which was also a space ship. The little air cooled engine in the boot seemed to scream rather loudly if Bobby took it over 50 miles an hour. So he just settled for a slow pootle of 45 up the M6. Bobby cared not a jot that his beloved VW Camper was being outperformed by every car on the road including the occasional Ford Anglia and even a Morris 1100. However, Bobby was buoyed with pride when he managed a successful overtake manoeuvre on a Hillman Imp.

At least with the reduced noise at lower speeds he could make out what Fanny was saying to him. Well he would have if Zoey, Mickey and Tallulah weren't screaming at each other, singing, bawling very loudly or kicking Bobby in the lower back repeatedly through the back of his seat repeating the mantra "Are we nearly there yet?" over and over! Bobby didn't mind though, he was a mellow chap and didn't get worked up about this kind of stuff, he liked to let it all wash over him…..and anyway Fanny would sort it all out in the end.

Zoey, like her mother, was very pretty and had shoulder length black shiny hair cut into a neat bob just like Fanny. She liked nothing more than to get dressed up in a pretty dress and have her hair neatly brushed and she liked to sing. She would listen to Fanny practising her show tunes and would quickly learn all the words and be able to sing them through unaided, often before Fanny had learned them herself.

Mickey, on the other hand, was a typical boy with tousled hair and a scruffy appearance most of the time, except of course when he was set upon by his mother and she would scrub the marks from his face with her moistened hanky, comb his hair into a neat side parting and straighten up his clothing. This was always a very temporary adjustment as within a few minutes Mickey had reverted to his natural self imposed disorderly state of dress and cleanliness.

Both Zoey and Mickey tolerated Tallulah. Tallulah got all the attention, being the baby. Well, she was a toddler now but she knew how to get noticed and it usually involved much screaming and constant inane chatter.

One very effective way of getting the kids attention and keeping them quiet for a few minutes, that Bobby adopted, was to tell the kids, "Prepare for 'Wing Deployment' and if we get up to 60 miles an hour we'll see if we can take off". He would press the 'Wing Deployment button' (which was actually just the ashtray) and the kids would stretch to peer over the doors to try and get a glimpse of the 'deployed' wings. Bobby would then call out the speed in increments of 1 mile an hour and when he finally managed to coax the struggling camper van to 60 with the engine screaming for mercy, Bobby would announce proudly, "We are up! We are flying! Can you see? Isn't it wonderful?" Zoey, Mickey and Tallulah really did believe that they were flying in the magic camper van.

Fanny very much took all the rumpus and chaos in her stride, she didn't seem to mind if the kids were making a noise, so long as they were happy and that just meant keeping them fed, watered, stimulated and having a nappy changed every now and then. Motherhood came naturally and she loved it, she loved life, she loved Bobby and most of all she loved her children. Fanny was a very special person though, all her life she had nurtured a passion for singing, dancing and musicals, she had big dreams and she was convinced that one day she would realise her destiny - one way or another.

So why then, you might ask, do we find our heroine, one of the main characters in our little story here, along with her family, travelling north, up the M6 away from London's West End? Just a holiday? Or was it something altogether more profound? Her dreams as yet unrealised, she, Fanny Blinkett, did not know. Nor did her young husband - Bobby.

Bang! With a violent jolt Fanny was wrenched from her daydreaming, the camper van lurched as it hit a pothole in the road. Fanny clutched her bump and she felt it kick ever so slightly and she smiled.

"Sorry my little honey bun", said Bobby as he gently laid his hand on her bump and he too felt a little kick. "So. Wot we gunna call the little bleeder then my darlin'?"

"Well", said Fanny, "If it's a girl Lavinia, and if it's a boy Elliot."

"Elliott, Elliott, you can't call the kid Elliott!" exclaimed Bobby. "Elliott is a fat kid with glasses who eats paste! No, you've got to give him a name like Elvis or Frank."

"Yeah, Sure thing Bobby", said Fanny.

Bobby was, of course, referring to the names of some of his best loved singers. Elvis Presley was by far his all time favourite and he was also a big fan of Frank Sinatra.

Bobby did like his music though and he also liked nothing more than dressing up as Elvis and singing some of his favourite Elvis songs at his local pub, 'The Dog and Duck' on a Saturday night. If they had had karaoke back then, then Bobby would have excelled. Instead he had to rely on the local band Simon and the Supersonics allowing him, as a favour, to take the mike on occasion and belt out some good old Elvis classics like 'It's now or Never', 'Teddy Bear', 'Jailhouse Rock' or 'Return to Sender' being a particular favourite with the locals. Sometimes Bobby would dress up as Elvis just for fun and take a walk down the high street in his white, sequin trimmed jump suit with the front zipped down to his waist revealing an over-hairy chest wig and sporting his gold rimmed sun-glasses.

They had turned off the M6 some way back and were now in the Scottish Borders and Bobby had slowed to a very sedate pace in order to take in the wonderful scenic countryside views. As he rounded a sweeping bend Bobby spied a beautiful looking little village set back from the main road and on the edge of the village there was the prettiest little house with a 'For Rent' sign outside.

"Cor blimey!" cried Bobby, "Look at that Aaaaas!" Unfortunately for Bobby, as he uttered this a rather well proportioned lady was bending down in the bus stop at the side of the road with her rear end pointing in the camper van's general direction.

Ka-slap! Was sound of the flat of Fanny's right hand meeting Bobby's left cheek at a rapid pace. "Stop looking at ladies bottoms Bobby and keep your eyes on the road," she said rather flatly.

Also unfortunately for Bobby 'Aaaaas' could be construed as two different things if you had a cockney accent. One was 'house' the other would was 'ass' or 'donkey'. Now Bobby knew what he meant and so do you and I, but Fanny, quite understandably, misunderstood her beloveds meaning and hence the rather undeserved skelp.

"Strike a light you daft mare. I said 'Aaaaas' not 'Aaaaas'! Look at that gorgeous little aaaaas with the for rent sign."

"Ooh, that IS lovely Bobby ……. I am sorry."

Bobby, with his face stinging, turned off the main road and brought the camper van to a halt outside the little house and surveyed its beautiful exterior. There was a name plate beside the front door which proclaimed "Rose Cottage".

You might say it was 'Chocolate box'. I wouldn't. I would just say it was a nice house.

The village itself was idyllic and across the road there was a free standing notice board within a kind of glass fronted cupboard. Fanny was drawn to it and slowly read out the most prominent of the notices, a rather untidy hand written poster. 'PANTOMIME' it proclaimed, 'IT'S PANTO AUDITION TIME'. Fanny smiled. She liked the sound of that. She quietly surveyed further the idyllic setting of the little hamlet. A little way off down the street was what appeared to be the village hall. The giveaway was the sign outside it which read 'Endersleigh Village Hall'.

Standing outside the village hall was a group of four men all sporting beards and all wearing tartan trews…. That's trousers to you and me. The four of them appeared to be observing, with interest, the goings-on at Rose Cottage. Fanny thought that this may have been the most activity they had observed for some time as nothing much else seemed to be happening. A stark contrast, she thought, to the hustle and bustle of her busy street in Bexleyheath.

Fanny did not really know why, but suddenly she felt absolutely certain that she and her family should get this house. This was where she wanted her family to live. It just felt right. Something inexplicable was happening to her, she felt some magical force urging her to move away from Bexleyheath, away from London where she had always thought her destiny lay. Fanny now felt, though, what was more important than her desire to be successful and famous was the best interests of her children and something was pulling her towards this place. She was sure that their futures lay here. She was sure that this decision was the most important decision she would make and she was making it on behalf of her family but mostly her unborn child.

Fanny turned to Bobby and very purposefully said, "This is where we should be, Bobby. This is where I want to be. Let's rent this house and live here."

"Wot!" said Bobby, a little surprised. "Sell up and move aaas, all the way from Bexley-Eef, up 'ere?"

Bobby was thinking hard. He could see that Fanny was serious. More than that, she was seriously serious and he could see that she wanted this house!

"All right then my little oil paintin', if that is wot you wanna do then that is wot we will do……Errr….. I can see about getting' a transfer up 'ere to the Scotland factory. I know they're looking for blokes to move up. It might even mean a promotion." Bobby had already convinced himself that it was a good idea.

Fanny continued to study the house and its pretty little garden and all the while Bobby was chattering away excitedly. She wasn't really listening to him any more as she knew she had him! It was in the bag as one might say. She knew Bobby wanted this too and he was just trying to justify the move to himself. He had a very logical, methodical brain and in his head he was already going through the process of making it happen. Fanny didn't want to listen as she knew in her head that it would happen. As Fanny was admiring the wee house she heard one of the four tartan clad spectators guffaw loudly as he presumably appreciated the punch line of one his associates' jokes. Bobby cast his gaze in their direction and said, "'Ere Darlin' those geeza's might know whose gaff this is. Jump back in the van and we'll go and ask 'em."

Fanny did just that and Bobby revved up the wee engine much more than was actually necessary to drive the thirty yards down the street. However, he wheel span away and skidded to an abrupt halt just level with group of, now silent, bearded gentlemen, all within the space of about five seconds. Bobby began to wind down the window to address the assembly but it stuck within three inches of the top of travel. Unperturbed, Bobby stretched his neck and tilted his head to address the four bemused chaps through the inadequate aperture.

"Good day my good fellows," Bobby put on his best posh accent, "Could you advise me of the whereabouts of the owner of this fine property and how one might go about rentin' it?"

The four men stared at Bobby blankly for a few seconds – it seemed longer – then they all leant in to the imagined centre point of their little group and began to debate the question posed and consider an appropriate response.

"What diddy say?" said one.

"Ah dinny ken," said another.

"Izzy French?" said the first again.

"Ah dinny ken," said the second again.

"Ah hink he's sellin' fish," said the third.

"Aye , these French fellas love thur fash. It'll no be bloody cheap mind."

"Aye, tell 'im naw," said the fourth.

The first of the four sidled cagily across to Bobby's, partly ajar, window and announced "Aye, wir no wantin' ony fash th' day pal." Whereupon he proudly returned to his friends and received a pat on the back from beardie number two, evidently, for the bravery of his actions.

Bobby was very confused by this little display. He had no idea what this man had just said to him. This was the first time he had encountered a Scotsman. He turned to Fanny who was sitting silently in the passenger seat and said "Stroof Fanny! These blokes are bleedin' barkin'!" He turned back and addressed the gap in the window once again with his initial query slightly rephrased in the interests of clarity for the four, who, to their credit, appeared to be concentrating intently and hanging on Bobby's every word. But to no avail, in unison they all shook their heads and huddled once more and were about to send forth their appointed spokesperson but were interrupted by Bobby throwing open the door of the van and striding purposefully to the rear of the vehicle. Bobby knew how to get the attention of this little lot and he had just the thing in the boot.

"Gordon Bennett! You would fink I was from the bleedin' Moon. Tell you wot Darlin'", he was addressing Fanny who was watching over the children in the back and thought it wise to let Bobby sort this little conundrum out himself, "I 'ave a right thirst," He said with a wink in her direction, "Fink I'll crack open a bottle o' sauce... A nice refreshing bottle o' Ferret's Armpit to wash away my troubles. Free my spirit of the cretinous tumult which we now find ourselves amidst. Yep. Nuffin' like a Ferret's armpit at times of stress." He reached into the, now open, rear door of the VW Campervans ample luggage storage compartment and withdrew a bottle of 'Armpit', deftly removed the top and glanced sideways at his tartan clad audience who were still standing, mouths agape towards the front of the van. He raised the bottle to his lips, closed his eyes and began to drain the contents of the bottle, savouring the taste of every drop of the amber nectar within. When he had eked out the last drops from the bottle he removed it from his lips and opened his eyes to find the four gentlemen closely huddled round him and the back of his vehicle. It seemed that the appearance of the ale bottle had evoked a primeval response within the group and Bobby now had their undivided attention. He surveyed the faces of the four, who were eagerly awaiting his next utterance.

"Can I interest you boys in a little Ferret's Armpit?" he said finally.

"Oh that would be very kind."

"Thank you very much."

"Dinny mind if ah dae."

The ease with which the group of four were now able to understand Bobby was truly astonishing. His little 'display' with the Ferret's Armpit had worked wonders. Fanny had known that Bobby had a talent for dealing with people. Some might say – playing them.

Anyway after a few jars of Armpit the group of chaps had, between them, become very chatty and had reported to Bobby and Fanny that Rose Cottage actually belonged to His Lordship. Lord Campbell-Endersleigh of Endersleigh Hall and the Endersleigh Estate. His Lordship pretty much owned everything for miles around Endersleigh, Endersleigh Estate was huge. Have I said Endersleigh enough yet? No! Well, Endersleigh Hall was at the far end of the village, up towards the moor... yes ....Endersleigh moor. It was the big house with round turrets - on a hill - overlooking the village. Some called it 'The Fairy Castle' as that is just what it looked like.

Bobby had introduced himself and his family to the four men, who by now, after two Armpits each, were close friends of Bobby, and they in turn reciprocated by introducing themselves to the new family in their midst.

They were – Harry McAbel, Harry McQuillin, Pat Cant and Walter Wilney.

The two Harrys had been friends since childhood and had grown up in Endersleigh. Harry McAbel had a very bushy ginger beard but black wavy hair. He was a farmer and had a very sharp sense of humour. He was a thoroughly nice, easy going chap and had a very calm demeanour. He and his wife worked one of the farms on the Endersleigh Estate. His wife, Mrs McAbel was a very strong willed, forthright and hard working woman. She stood for no nonsense from anyone and she kept Harry in check. She was well able to pull her weight on the farm and was well organised. She was also a very generous and caring person. However, the farm wasn't all that profitable they only just managed to eke a living out of it and were by no means as rich as all the fancy four-by-four driving farmers of the neighbouring counties. Apparently it was a similar story for all the farmers of the Endersleigh Estate but the two Harrys offered no explanation as to what the nature of the difficulties were, other than describing them as unexplained losses.

Harry McQuillin had a lovely white beard and a bit of a beer belly. He had worked in the coalmines at the nearby Newtongrunge pit until it was closed some 25 years ago and he had never worked since. He had, though, managed to secure a sizeable pay-out prior to the closure on health grounds! He would say no more than this. He did look extremely healthy though – it had to be said, apart from a very slight limp which most thought he was putting on! As a result he never had to work again and this suited him just fine. He was a bit of a practical joker though and you had to be on your guard as he liked to wind people up. His wife, Mrs McQuillin was a very popular person in the village. She was liked by all and was very easy going and seemed to accept without question the antics of her beloved Harry. The two Harrys (McAbel and McQuillin) were collectively known in the village as 'Able and Willin' and it had caused a few chuckles within the villagers when their wee clique was swelled with the addition of Pat Cant and Walter Wilney or 'Canny and Wilney'. These two never seemed to work either and had been dubbed 'Canny work and Wilney work' by the guy in the village who made up the nicknames – every village has one! The truth was though that Canny and Wilney were Pools winners. The Pools was like the seventies version of the lottery. You had to guess eight football matches that were going to end in a draw on Saturday – it had to be a score draw though because you got three points for a score draw and only two for a no-score-draw. Twenty four points was like getting six numbers in the lottery. You could win big! And Pat and Walter had done it. They had chosen, though, to remain anonymous, collected the money and moved to Endersleigh from the city. They were very close friends and chose to live together. Wilney was tall and thin and was always meticulously dressed and kept his beard neatly trimmed at all times whereas Canny was really quite short and slight but with a little bit of a belly and was scruffy in comparison. He was a little less concerned with his appearance and often had the remnants of breakfast lodged in his scruffy beard or down his front.

Anyway, Canny and Wilney moved in to the village and had become very good friends with Able and Willin. They all liked a drink (as was evident to Bobby) and every Friday night they would sit in Canny and Wilney's shed at the bottom of the garden on the edge of the village enjoying a few ales and each other's company. They would raise the flag at the side of the shed to indicate that they were 'in residence' and many of the villagers, on seeing the flag up, would bring along a bottle or two and share a libation with the four friends. Many a raucous Friday night was spent in the shed. They were a very sociable crowd.

Fanny and Bobby had warmed to the four gents and were enthused by their assertions that Endersleigh was a very close, welcoming and inclusive community. They said their farewells and headed in the direction of Endersleigh Hall.

Chapter 4

Bloomers and Pantyhose

The little yellow and white camper van chugged up the hill to the front of the very impressive looking Endersleigh Hall. It had a very large oak door, either side of which were circular tower turrets with slit windows. It wasn't at all symmetrical and in fact seemed a little higgledy-piggledy with a larger and immensely high circular turret to the left of centre and the building took on a more regular rectangular form on the right side with a Georgian façade. This wing extending out sufficiently for eight substantial windows to be accommodated along its length and sufficiently high to contain three full storey's and an extra storey within the ample roof space. All in all though Fanny thought it was a very beautifully proportioned building which was pleasing on the eye.

Bobby pulled up outside the huge oak door. There were no other vehicles or indeed any signs of life evident at this side of the building, which made Fanny think that perhaps they ought to go round the back. Presumably they would have a tradesman's entrance for less eminent visitors such as them.

By now though Bobby had already made his way up the grand steps and banged the very large door knocker in the shape of a lion's head. It made a very loud, echoing bang which seemed to resound within the cavernous interior of the large house.

Fanny had removed the children from the van and had sat Tallulah on her hip with one arm round her while she shepherded the two older children up the steps. On reaching the massive door Zoey and Mickey pleaded with Bobby to allow them to have a go with the huge lion head knocker. Bobby duly obliged and lifted them up in turn, Mickey first. Zoey was having her go when all of a sudden came the unexpectedly loud bang of the door being unbolted from inside. It gave them all quite a start, not least Zoey who on reaching terra-firma again scampered in behind her mum's skirt.

The door then slowly swung open to reveal two unusual looking butlers. At least, Bobby assumed they were butlers as this is what their attire suggested. They both wore dark morning suit jackets and pinstripe trousers, high necked white shirts with fly-away collars and bow ties. The butler who seemed to be standing to the front of the two was quite a tall chap with a prominent hooked nose and had a very pompous air about him. He stood very erect. The second butler, in contrast, was much shorter but this was largely due to the fact that he was stooping badly as if he were suffering from some kind of serious back ailment! He also seemed to be standing behind the first butler lifting his head only occasionally to survey the scene or to glance at his colleague, the remainder of the time surveying the ground to the rear of him. He was quite stocky with a shock of thick, black hair which was pressed into an untidy side parting with an excessive amount of some kind of hair product.

Fanny thought them a very peculiar pair.

"Yes, can I help you?" asked the lead butler.

"Can vee 'elp you?" asked the other in what seemed to be a rather thick German accent.

"Good day to you good sirs," Bobby was again adopting his best posh accent, "Would it be possible, at all, to discuss with His Lordship the matter of Rose Cottage wot we noticed, not 'alf an hour ago, was up for rent? We would like to convey to His Lordship our interest in rentin' it, if the price is right of course. Izzy in?"

After an elongated pause the lead butler let out a low moaning sigh which was immediately copied by the trailing, stooping butler and as they began to turn away the front one said in a most pompous manner. "Very well, walk this way, wipe your feet and keep those children at heel."

"Vipe your feet unt keep zee kinder close."

Fanny thought them most rude and was about to reprimand them by pointing out that they were children not dogs but thought it perhaps better to hold her tongue on this occasion.

As the two butlers swung round to lead the way Bobby and Fanny were dumbstruck by the manner in which the pair moved. As the tall, lead butler turned the stooping, following butler wheeled round behind him maintaining his position relative to the leading butler's posterior. Then they moved off in unison at a trot.

As the peculiar duo trotted ahead, Bobby too broke into a trot and pretended to grip imaginary reins, being careful not to be seen and cast a cheeky grin back in Fanny's direction. She was following at a fast walk with Tallulah on her hip and resisted the temptation break into a trot. Zoey and Mickey however showed none of their mother's restraint and settled into a fast and very loud canter accompanied by whinnies and neighs for good measure. The butlers evidently oblivious to the shenanigans behind them pulled up at a large door at the far end of the great hall. They wheeled round to face the advancing Blinkett's who quickly dropped their equine tomfoolery and walked to a standing stop.

The pair then turned to face the door and the lead butler first knocked and without waiting for a response threw open the double doors. The duo took a few strides into the room and the lead butler announced, "Someone to see you Milord."

"Some vun to see you, mein Herr," said the other.

"Well, show them in Withers, show them in!" The tall, lead butler, evidently named Withers, beckoned the young family to enter his Lordship's parlour.

They all marched in and were met, yet again, by a very peculiar scene! His Lordship was not at all what any one of them had been expecting! He was standing by a large full length mirror with his back to the door. He seemed to be putting the finishing touches to the elaborate make-up on his face. He had bright red lipstick on large bow-shaped lips, exaggeratedly large false eye lashes, mascara, eye liner, bright red rouge on his cheeks and glitter all over his face. He was also wearing a hairnet but there didn't seem to be much in the way of hair inside it. This, in itself, was quite surprising enough, but it didn't end there. His Lordship was wearing, on the upper part of his body, a body suit sporting a very buxom pair of bosom's neatly packed into a very fetching pink polka-dot bikini top whilst his lower half was clad in stockings (possibly American tan) and a pair of green polka-dot bloomers elasticated in at the knee. He was indeed a very peculiar sight.

Bobby and Fanny stood agape before him and Zoey and Mickey both nervously reached for their mummy's free hand.

"Mummy, why is the man dressed as a lady?" Nothing escaped Zoey's attention!

"Ah-ha!" he roared as he spun round. "What a sweet little child. You are a little cutie aren't you?" He said as he approached Zoey and attempted to tousle her hair but Zoey had slid behind her mum's skirts again in order to escape the clutches of this madman.

"Where are my manners?" He shouted. "I am His Lordship – Lord Avery Campbell-Endersleigh. I see that you have met my two loyal menservants Withers and Hock. Forgive my attire but tonight is village panto audition night and I am hoping for the role of the Pantomime Dame. I have just been reading through the script and trying on my new dame outfit. I do like to dress to impress at the auditions. It seems to be a very successful tactic." He began to guffaw loudly. He certainly had a very loud, brusque and confident manner about him and it made Fanny a little uneasy.

What His Lordship had neglected to say was that it was a given that he would be the panto dame this year as he was every year. Other men in the village had tried to audition for the role but had invariably met with unexplained misfortunes, obviously instigated by His Lordship, which rendered them unable to audition and hence His Lordship's desire to always be the Endersleigh panto dame was fulfilled year after year. Similarly, His Lordship insisted that Withers and Hock would always be the pantomime horse. This could, perhaps, explain the peculiar behaviour of his two menservants. They always behaved as if in pantomime horse costume but what was not clear was whether this was an elaborate method acting rehearsal strategy deployed to enhance pantomime performances OR whether this was their normal demeanour. Hock's severe stoop however certainly leant itself to making him an ideal candidate to play the horse's ass.

"As you can see, I am a very busy man." His Lordship continued. "May I enquire who you are and what is the nature of your enquiry? In short, state your name and your business man! Come on, pip-pip!" He, evidently, was addressing Bobby who was still trying to make sense of this vision before him. He quickly snapped out of it and addressed the peculiar Peer.

"Well Your Lordship, we would very much like to rent yer aaaas!" said Bobby.

"He means your house your Lordship, your HOUSE!" Fanny interjected. She wanted to avoid any confusion.

"That is to say, yer 'ighness, Rose Cottage - in the village. We would like to rent Rose Cottage", explained Bobby.

"Well that very much depends." said His Lordship whose tone and volume had lowered and whose countenance darkened somewhat. He moved in close to study Bobby's face from an inch away. Bobby felt a little uncomfortable and leant back, away from the nose-to-nose contact he was enduring and swallowed uneasily, "Rose Cottage is only for rent to the right people - people who will integrate into this very close community. We don't want any weirdoes in Endersleigh."

Bobby and Fanny surveyed His Lordship and then Withers and Hock and both secretly concurred that there certainly was no room in Endersleigh for any more weirdoes. They returned their gazes to His Lordship and both nodded in agreement.

"Tell me a little about yourselves." His Lordship continued.

Fanny began to relay at length a précis of who they were, of their history and interests, in particular her love and knowledge of theatre and the stage. She told him of Bobby's love for music. She expressed her hopes for their children's futures and she expressed her desire to integrate into this rural community and make a home for her family. His Lordship listened intently, expressionless. It would have been difficult to perceive any kind of expression change from under the thick covering of comedy make-up anyway.

"Yes, that's all very well young lady but I would expect the successful prospective tenants of Rose Cottage to make………. sacrifices!"

"Sacrifices???" Bobby and Fanny said together shakily and there followed an uneasy, elongated pause while His Lordship revelled in the extrapolation of their discomfort.

"Yes, I will insist that you take part in the annual village pantomime, we are very proud of our long and glorious thespian heritage here in Endersleigh and past successes and accolades which go back years and years, I think that the village could use someone like you."

Fanny and Bobby both sighed with relief.

"Ooh yes," said Fanny, "I would be delighted to your Lordshipness."

"Of course there are certain understandings that are a given. The main one being that yours truly here is, and always will be, the Pantomime Dame. It's a sort of tradition you see. The villagers love it and wouldn't have it any other way." He engaged Bobby with an intense stare and added.

"Do we understand each other Blinkett?"

"Oh, absolutely, yer 'ighness. I 'ave no interest in wearing frocks whatsoever. I like to leave that kind of fing to the ladies......."

Fanny dug her elbow into Bobby's ribs, fearing that he was about to insult His Lordship, and he winced. He got the message though. He should stop talking immediately.

"...... and blokes wot dress up as panto dames.... Elvis is my fing."

"Excellent. Ha haha", bellowed His Lordship evilly.

"So we can 'ave the Aaaaaaaas?" said Bobby.

His Lordship turned away and shouted loudly "Withers and Hock will run through the legals with you. Goodbye. Withers, Hock see them to the door."

"Yes, Mi'Lord."

"Ja, mein Herr."

It all ended rather abruptly and Fanny and Bobby were a little stuck for words so said nothing as they were shepherded out of the parlour. They were, however, fairly satisfied that they had achieved their objective.

Now to make it happen.

Chapter 5

New Pants and Tutus

After all the boring legal stuff was dealt with and Bobby had organised that transfer through his work they made the final arrangements for the move. Bobby and Fanny had said their goodbyes to all their friends in Bexleyheath, they had packed all their belongings into boxes for the removals guys to pack away into the big lorry and they said a last farewell to the little house that had been home for, what seemed like, an age now. Fanny's excitement was certainly tinged with a little sadness at the prospect of never seeing this place again! For Zoey, Mickey and Tallulah though it was just a big exciting adventure.

When they arrived back in Endersleigh on the day of the move they were greeted by an unexpected welcoming party! Able and Willin had arranged for a whole bunch of locals to help move the new, young family in to Rose Cottage and give them a good old Endersleigh welcome.

Canny and Wilney were busy with something else that day.

It was noted by some of the other helpers that there wasn't an awful lot of lifting and carrying going on with Able and Willin and more organising and directing. Willin said it was on account of his condition though and Able said he was just being sociable and would get to it forthwith, which he eventually did.

Fanny, being the very organised type of person that she was, had labelled all the boxes to indicate what was in them and which room they should be put in and it wasn't long before the big removals lorry was emptied and was tooting its goodbye with everyone waving after it as it pulled away out of the village.

Able and Willin had brought along their wives who were excellent workers and seemed to know instinctively what needed to be done. Mrs McQuillin set about setting up the kiddies bedrooms, getting the beds assembled with the help of one of the young lads from the village who had pitched up to help. It was important, she said, that the kids had a stable base from the word go, somewhere where they felt safe and at home with familiar things surrounding them and she wasn't at all annoyed by Zoey and Mickey emptying boxes and boxes of toys in the middle of the floor of their room as she was trying get it in a liveable state for them! She had found the box labelled 'kid's linen' and worked away at getting the beds made up and not a moment too soon it seemed as no sooner had she announced the beds complete that Zoey and Mickey began to bounce up and down on them for a few minutes before finally succumbing to fatigue and they both cowped fairly quickly. Fanny had been watching and had guessed that nap time was approaching fast and she thanked Mrs McQuillin for seeing to the needs of the kids so instinctively and proficiently. It was all becoming a bit overwhelming for Fanny and she felt herself becoming a little emotional but was able to hide it and just carried on with all the things that just needed to be done.

Mrs McAbel had given herself the unenviable task of getting the kitchen in some kind of order. She was quite a formidable woman (it was plain to see who wore the trousers in her house) and was barking orders at some of the fit, strong young men who were lifting into place all the big appliances - cooker, twin-tub, refrigerator and the like and they got them working as quick as you like! As soon as Mrs McAbel had found the kettle and cups she was busily making tea for all the helpers. She had brought all the ingredients in the tractor with her in a wicker shopping bag from which she also produced a massive homemade chocolate cake.

Everyone stopped for tea and cake.

It was not long after that that Rose Cottage began to look very much more like a home than a bombsite and Fanny was feeling so much happier about things. She really truly felt the warmest gratitude to all the people of Endersleigh who had turned up to help them get settled in. She had had a big day and had directed this whole operation while balancing a very ratty Tallulah on her hip and also being very, very pregnant.

Everything that could be done had been done by early evening and Bobby made a very heartfelt speech thanking his new friends and neighbours for all their efforts and making their arrival in Endersleigh a most special occasion. He invited them to stay for a few beers and a sing song and cracked open a few bottles of Ferret's Crotch. Pretty much everyone had declined and made their excuses and left them to it. They genuinely did have stuff to do. But Able and Willin were eager to join Bobby for a 'swift one' and had despatched their respective wives in the direction of home with assurances that they would not 'overstay their welcome', nor 'make fools of themselves'.

Ever so coincidentally, Canny and Wilney pitched up just as the first beer was getting decanted. They extended their apologies that they had been unable to help as there was this huge problem that they had had to deal with and they were late as a result….. But yes, they would love to stay for 'swift half'.

A swift one and a swift half multiplied into many more Ferret's Crotches and Ferret's Armpits and Bobby toasted the chaps their good health with a bottle of 25 year old Glen McToshan Malt Whisky. The Tartan Trews chaps all toasted Bobby, who was by now sporting his Elvis gear as he had found the box with it in. Then they toasted Fanny with more Glen McToshan and then they toasted His Lordship and his faithful menservants Withers and Hock with the last drops of Bobby's treasured 25 year old Glen McToshan which he had kept safe in his drinks cabinet for many years, saving it for a special occasion. This, it seemed, was it.

Able and Willin staggered home to face the wrath of their respective wives with their assurances in tatters. Canny and Wilney just staggered home.

It was only two days later that it happened.

Bobby was at work, having just started the day previous in his new position at the greetings card factory. He had just thought up the most amazing joke for one of his new line of Condolence Cards when he received the message.

"Waters broken - get home quick." Given that it is still 1977 and text messages had not yet been invented, you might be wondering what medium was used for the transmission of this message. Bobby was wondering too.

He had just been handed a piece of paper with the message on it. It could've been a transcribed phone call or a telegram. No, wait...... If that were the case then it would've read "Waters broken stop get home quick stop" and it didn't. Hang on a minute! Yes, that's it! Fax machines had just been invented. But, wait. No. He didn't have a fax machine. They cost thousands of pounds and he was poor. Bobby pondered over this question for a good few minutes before suddenly coming to his senses and realising the urgency and gravity of the situation. He rushed home as fast as the wee campervan would take him stopping only once - at the betting shop. It was his last chance to place that bet on the 4.30 at Musselburgh for Able and Willin. 'Kick in the Sporran' was a dead cert with long odds. How often do you hear that? Not often I'll wager. It was too good an opportunity to miss.

Bobby screeched to a halt outside Rose cottage. Able's tractor was parked there also. Able and Willin were standing by the front door. Able was pacing up and down and hurriedly rushed towards the van to greet Bobby.

" Now dinae you fuss Boaby. A 'hing's gauny be fine and dandy. Mrs McAbel is wi' 'er an' a 'hink Mrs Willin an' a'. On ye gan up man."

Bobby had no clue what Able had just said but got the gist of it. He rushed in the front door and Mrs McQuillin who was tending to the kids in the kitchen pointed up to the ceiling indicating that that was where all the action was going on. Bobby climbed the stairs, the door to the main bedroom was closed. Bobby stopped and put his ear to the door. "Strange," he thought. "Nothing!"

Bobby had attended a few of these gigs before and they were usually noisy, quite messy affairs, so, unusual to be so quite, he thought. He slowly opened the door and squeezed his head past it to see what was going on......

Fanny had felt a bit funny that morning after Bobby had left for work. She had started to feel the odd kick. Nothing too unusual about that she thought. Then, a little while later it all started to get a little crazy. It felt like there was a stampede going on in her tummy. Much more than she had experienced before. She was a little concerned so she telephoned up to Mingingshaw Farm and spoke to Mrs McAbel who immediately rushed to Rose Cottage with her other half at the helm. 'Rushed' is probably too strong a word. Mr and Mrs McAbel travelled everywhere in their cab-less 1964 Massey-Fergusson 135 tractor. It was their only means of transport and rushing anywhere was a tall order! Suffice to say they got there as quickly as they could under the circumstances.

Able was ordered to wait outside and Mrs McAbel went in. Fanny was standing in the kitchen rubbing her bump looking a little anxious with the children playing quietly at the table. Mrs McQuillin arrived soon after and the two helped Fanny upstairs to her room to lie down. Mrs McQuillin returned downstairs to look after the children.

"Now you just lie there dear there's no need to worry," said Mrs McAbel, "I'll just go and give Dr Finlayson a call and get him to come and check you over."

"Oh, I'm sure it's fine Mrs McAbel. Thank you. It's so kind of you."

"Och! Not at all Lassie. Dinnae be daft. It's no bother at all. I'll be back in a jiffy."

Mrs McAbel rose and turned to exit the room and was about to reach for the door handle when...... POOF! (Hopefully, in this age of political correctness, POOF! is still an acceptable expletive to indicate a sort of magical explosion – if not then please accept my apologies and have...... no......... there is nothing else ..... It's going to have to be POOF!)

POOF!

There was a flash and smoke and a whooshing poof noise, Fanny got quite a start, and the smoke cleared to reveal, standing by Fanny's bedside the unmistakable form of a Fairy. A FAIRY GODMOTHER! Was Fanny dreaming? Was she having some kind of breakdown? She closed her eyes tight and opened them again. She was still there - The Fairy Godmother! Yes it was THE Fairy

Godmother Fanny now remembered she had fleetingly seen at her wedding.

"Hello little girl, remember me? I'm your Fairy Godmother."

"Have you got the right house? I don't have a Fairy Godmother. And what have you done with Mrs McAbel?" Fanny had just noticed that Mrs McAbel was frozen in the same position, reaching for the door handle.

"Oh, she'll be fine. I just needed to have a little private chat with you before we move on with your wish", said the Fairy Godmother.

"Wish! What wish?" Said Fanny feeling a little uncomfortable - if not shocked.......

....

Christmas 1957 - Nether Wallop near Reading.

The little girl knelt on the mat at the front of the village hall with her chin resting on the edge of the stage staring up at the very colourful spectacle of the Ugly Sisters eagerly trying to squeeze their oversized feet into the dainty glass slipper. The girl's aunt, her mum's sister, had insisted that she and her mother should come out to her place for the weekend and they should all go and see the Nether Wallop Christmas pantomime which was always excellent. This year it was Cinderella. She had been so excited to be going to see a real pantomime. She hadn't been to one before. Perhaps, she thought, they didn't have pantomime's in London. She was so glad she had come though as it was the best thing she had ever seen. She was loving it. She was totally engrossed in the story and was fully invested in assisting Cinderella and her allies in any way she could. She was very noisily shouting "Behind you!" when it was required or joining in with the "Oh no it isn't!" and equally noisily booing at Cinderella's evil stepmother whenever she appeared. She was enchanted by the beauty of the pantomime horse and thought it the most magnificent horse she had ever seen, although she hadn't actually seen a real horse before - only pictures in books. It was white with dapples of brown and had a very friendly face, although it did have a rather fixed bemused expression pretty much all of the time.

The Ugly Sisters had each tried and failed to put on the magic glass slipper and now it was Cinderella's turn.

The beautiful Fairy Godmother, who had the whitest fairy wings and a sparkly wand with a star shaped end and a tiara and a very full pom-pom shaped tutu, addressed all the children at the front. "Do you think it will fit Cinderella children?" she asked.

"Yeeessss", they all screamed.

"Would someone like to come up here and help Cinderella try on the glass slipper?"

In a flash the little girl had jumped to her feet and thrust her hand as high up in the air as it would go. She was on her tiptoes, determined to be the one the Fairy Godmother chose.

"Well", said the Fairy Godmother, "I think this little girl here should come and help Cinderella try on the slipper."

She was overjoyed and on the stage in an instant and with the help of the Fairy Godmother and closely observed by the pantomime horse she was able to slide the glass slipper onto Cinderella's foot. This was possibly the best moment of the girl's life for now she knew that Cinderella would be able to marry the handsome Prince and free herself from her life of toil and grime at the hands of her wicked stepmother. There followed raucous applause from the packed-in audience and the little girl stood and observed all the joy filled faces of the people in the crowd until there was silence. Then the Fairy Godmother turned to her and said, "You have been so helpful little girl, I will grant you a wish. What will it be?"

At that moment an usherette walked out from the wing to centre stage. I say 'usherette', it was actually a rather burly bearded man wearing an usherette costume complete with fishnets and high heels. She.... I mean - he was carrying a tray, usherette style with a strap supporting the tray looped round the back of her....... I mean - his neck, containing three items. A bar of chocolate, a bag of cheese and onion flavoured crisps and a bottle of pop. The Fairy Godmother presented the array of goodies by wafting the open palm of her free hand in front of the tray as if to say "This is your choice for your wish".

The little girl looked at the Fairy Godmother and then to the selection of goodies on offer which were rather unappealing to her, it had to be said. She looked to the audience and sought out her mother's face smiling up at her. She then looked back and pointed in the direction of the glamorous usherette and said "I want one of those." However it wasn't anything on the tray she was pointing at, she was pointing past the usherette to the pantomime horse who was standing at the back of the stage. The pantomime horse whose bemused expression turned to one of panic as all eyes turned to him, shifted his stance uneasily.

There was silence in the hall. A man coughed nervously. Chairs creaked as buttock cheeks were shifted uncomfortably.

"So it's a pantomime horse you want?" said the Fairy Godmother.

"Yes," said the girl, still clearly pointing at the pantomime horse, "When I grow up, I want one of those and I will call him Pants."

The audience exploded into fits of laughter and the Fairy Godmother with a wry smile and a shake of her head gently caressed the girls head with the tip of the wand and said "OK then, little girl, your wish is granted." She then released and handful of magic fairy dust over the head of the girl, who looked up into the magical cloud, closed her eyes and made her wish once more.

....

"Oh Fanny! You must remember the wish you made in Nether Wallop when you were a little girl. You wanted to have a…….."

"Pantomime horse," said Fanny finishing her sentence for her. "You are kidding of course." She now remembered, in full, her first encounter with the Fairy Godmother. There were so many things going on in Fanny's head. So many questions. Was this person real? Were there really Fairy Godmothers? Were wishes real? Could wishes be granted? Who invented fried food and why? Were Pantomime Horses real? If so what had she done to deserve this? What was going to happen now?

"That's right Fanny. You're going to have a baby pantomime horse!"

"Whoa! Hold on there just one minute Mrs Fairy Godmother. I am the mother of three children. I have been here before. It's not normally no walk in the park - poppin' out a bleedin' normal baby and you are seriously telling me I'm about to squeeze out a bloomin' horse! You must be bonkers!"

"Don't fret now Fanny I have sent a message to Bobby, he's on his way, this'll be easy. This'll be a magic birth. You won't feel a thing and then all will be as normal....well as normal as it can be bringing up a pantomime horse"

"Also, I would like to point out that I was only bleedin' six years old when I made that wish."

"A wish is a wish Fanny and I am bound by the Fairy Godmother's code, and you did make that wish didn't you Fanny? And as I recall it was one of the most sincere wishes that I had the pleasure of receiving and now granting. Of course these things can't be considered lightly. This is a serious undertaking, a massive responsibility and I had to wait till you were ready. Now you are ready Fanny. It's going to be really great Fanny and you are going to love PANTS!"

"Whoa, whoa! Pants?"

"Pants is his name, Fanny. That is what you named him when you made your wish. He's a little boy, Fanny, a beautiful little boy. This is a magical place and Pants will be happy here. This is why you are here. You must love him Fanny and I will be watching."

Fanny was about to remonstrate a little more with the, clearly deranged, Fairy Godmother when……

POOF!

The big whooshing poof happened again and the Fairy Godmother vanished in a puff of smoke. Mrs McAbel unfroze and turned to Fanny, apparently unaware that anything weird had just happened, and said "There you go, Fanny, my dear. That was easy wasn't it?"

"Was it? What was?" Fanny thought.

Mrs McAbel reached down into the crib at Fanny's bedside and lifted out Fanny's new baby and presented to Fanny the littlest most beautiful pantomime horse that she had ever seen. He was fast asleep and had a cute little horsey face with tiny pointed ears laying flat to his head. His body was white linen with two brown dapples either side and his four little legs, clothed in grey stripy cotton, dangled helplessly as Mrs McAbel handed over the sleeping baby boy. He had little black baby booties on his little baby feet – not hooves – feet.

"Looks like you've got yourself a lovely little boy, Fanny", said Mrs McAbel.

"Oh, he is beautiful Mrs McAbel isn't he?" said Fanny who now had no pregnancy bump. She took the baby pantomime horse in her arms and snuggled and he snuggled back. All the doubts that Fanny had had in her head vanished in that instant and she knew that this was her baby and she loved him. She knew what the fairy godmother had meant, in that, this is a magical place. There was no doubt that Pants was different from other children but Fanny knew that in this place those differences would not matter.

At that moment Bobby stuck his head round the door. "Got 'ere as quick as I could my little pumpkinseed." Bobby entered the room and approached his beloved who was holding the newest member of the Blinkett family. "Well, who have we got 'ere then?" Bobby tenderly clapped or stroked or patted whatever you do to a baby pantomime horse.

"It's a little boy Bobby," said Fanny.

"You are a beautiful little lad aren't you my boy," cooed Bobby. He too had never seen a more beautiful pantomime horse. In truth Bobby had never seen a pantomime horse in his life but that didn't seem to matter. This one was theirs and they were going to love him to bits.

"So, have you got a name in mind then?" asked Mrs McAbel.

"Yes Mrs McAbel," said Fanny. "This is PANTS! Pants Blinkett."

Able and Willin had been patiently waiting outside and had been trying to pass the time with a game of 'I spy'. As Able was dyslexic and Willin had chosen something that he couldn't see anyway, Willin had won quite easily. Able went into one of his huffs and accused Willin of cheating. So Willin came up with a new game. It was called 'Guess the gender of Boaby's new baby', which was fairly self explanatory. To spice it up there was ten bob to the winner. They made their choices and wrote them on a scrap of paper each and waited for the news to emerge from within Rose Cottage. It did eventually in the form of Bobby and they both anxiously looked at him and Willin could wait no longer. "Well Bobby. What is it?" He asked.

"It's a little baby Harry", said Bobby stating the bloomin' obvious thought Willin and Able. "It's a little baby……. pantomime horse!"

"Aw Bugger!" They said in unison and both ripped up their makeshift betting slips. Neither of them had seen that coming! There was always the 4.30 at Musselburgh.

Chapter 6

Training Pants

Part 1 - 3 Hands

The new baby, Pants, slept for most of the next day. Fanny was up and about cleaning and tidying, tending to the other 3 children's needs and didn't have much time to think about anything. She was aware, however, that she felt remarkably well considering she had just 'given birth' to a bouncing baby pantomime horse the day before. On previous occasions she had needed about a week to recover.

Zoey, Mickey and Tallulah were really excited to have a new baby brother and were keen to take a peek while he was still sleeping in the crib.

"Cool!" said Mickey. "When can we play with him mum?"

"Let him sleep," said Fanny, "perhaps tomorrow."

The next day was a big day.

Pantomime horse's, like real horses, learn to stand and walk pretty much straight away. This is basically a defence mechanism so that they can run from dangers in the wild like lions, tigers and wolves. Fortunately, there were none of these in Endersleigh but nevertheless it remained a priority for Pants to be on his feet as soon as possible. It wasn't long before he was striving to attain this objective.

The very first time he tried it, he went for his front legs first but got the angle wrong and did front leg splits with his back legs still in the seated position. Then he thought - back legs first might be the way to go, so he pushed his bottom up high into the air with his legs extended as far as they could go, but unfortunately had his feet too close together and toppled sideways into a heap. A couple more unsuccessful attempts later Pants decided the way to go was - front first with legs apart followed closely by back feet, legs apart, head down looking backwards between legs so as to keep track of what was going on down below. Once up, he would slowly raise his head till fully erect. Job done! Pants was a quick learner and had soon perfected this and swiftly moved on to 'walking in a straight line'. Not so simple as it sounds! But, after a few comedy, drunk man attempts had perfected this also. Pants was very keen to show off his new skills to the assembled Blinkett's, and after a few bungled attempts and comedy tumbles managed to pull off a perfect ten to huge applause from them all.

Pants spent all his time over the next few days practising his sitting, standing and walking skills in the garden under the watchful eye of Fanny. She was amazed with the speed at which Pants was developing his skills. With Pantomime Horses, she suddenly realised, there really was no 'helpless baby stage'. Things seemed to be moving apace, which was a shame, as every new mum likes to take a walk with the baby in the pram to proudly show off the new arrival. Perhaps, she thought, she needed to do this sooner rather than later.

Fanny still had all Mickey and Tallulah's baby clothes and pram bedding and after a brief search found an old blue romper suit of Mickey's. So, in an attempt to present little Pants at his best, she carefully cut out the back of the romper suit and pulled it on Pants' front half but the sleeves were hanging loose, which Fanny thought looked a little odd. So she stuffed each sleeve with a couple of pairs of Bobby's rolled up socks from the laundry pile. It was the best she could manage at such short notice. She decided just to leave his back end 'au naturale'. She bundled him into the pram, tucked him in tightly so only his head was visible over the rain guard and under the hood and headed up the street to the shop and post office, with the three other kids reluctantly trailing behind. There was bound to be someone around she could show off her Pants to.

There was. Old Mrs Milligan was just coming out of the post office just as Fanny rounded the corner.

"Oh, your new baby Mrs Blinkett! Ye dinnae mind if I have a wee peek?" she cooed as she fished in her purse for 10p to push under the baby's pillow.

"Not at all Mrs Milligan", said Fanny proudly as she stopped just short of the elderly lady.

Now Pants hadn't exactly been happy with being bundled into the pram, bound in a romper suit and sheets and carted off up the street for no good reason and had been planning his Houdini-like escape from the outset. He had already managed to work himself free of the tightly bound sheets and saw his opportunity to break for freedom as Mrs Milligan's big beaming face appeared over the rain guard after unclipping it.

To Fanny's horror, and to Zoey, Mickey and Tallulah's glee, Pants leapt to his feet (which was very impressive for someone who had only mastered rising to the standing position and walking in straight lines a few day previously) and jumped on top of the pram's principal sleeping compartment and began to buck like a 'bucking bronco' with his makeshift arms flailing in a demented fashion in an attempt to shake off the bizarre romper suit which, alas, ultimately turned out to be unsuccessful.

Mrs Milligan's expression of friendly adoration quickly vanished and was replaced by one of sheer horror. She let out an ear piercing scream and cried "Whi'ss-'at-coming-oot-'is-erse?"

You could see her point, thought Fanny, it did look for all the world that some abnormal white appendage was protruding from the rear end of the blue romper suit.

In retrospect, as Mrs Milligan turned and ran away down the street screaming, Fanny's realised that her foolhardy attempt to temporarily and hastily dress Pants had been ill advised.

She grabbed Pants, mid bounce, and returned him to his sleeping quarters, turned and hurriedly headed for home with her entourage, sadly regretting the whole sorry incident.

Mrs Milligan, however, had taken temporary refuge in the Police Station to escape the clutches of the demented beast which had attacked her and it transpired that she had lodged a complaint with the village policeman PC Caruthers to that effect.

38

PC Caruthers was a little on the porky side it had to be said, in fact he was quite probably wider than he was tall and he struggled to make any kind of movement without becoming very out of puff within a few steps. It was probably fortunate for him that there weren't many criminals in Endersleigh that needed chasing down. It wasn't long before PC Caruthers came waddling out of the police station with a very ashen faced Mrs Milligan cowering behind pointing in the direction of Fanny who was just getting back in through the garden gate to Rose Cottage. Fanny saw them coming and tried to explain to the pair what had happened and tried to offer Mrs Milligan an apology but PC Caruthers began to lecture Fanny on 'antisocial behaviour' and terrorising the local community with unruly children and pets. This sort of behaviour, he had said, was not acceptable in Endersleigh and that if there were any further incidents then he would have no hesitation in having them evicted and ejected from the village as he had the power to do so ….. AND the full support of His Lordship.

Fanny ushered the children back into the house, fuming. She was obviously quite embarrassed by the incident but felt that there had been a slight over-reaction on the parts of both Mrs Milligan and the fat and very rude village Bobby. She took an instant dislike to him and their paths rarely crossed from then on. However he became a constant thorn in the sides of Bobby and the boys whenever they were trying to enjoy a few beers in the garden or in the hut by threatening Antisocial Behaviour Orders and charges of Breach of the Peace. No-one in the village was complaining, it was just the obese PC exercising his authority and being a pain in the proverbial.

Following the regrettable 'Mrs Milligan incident' Fanny had thought it best to get busy making some proper clothes for Pants. So she hunted out the old sewing machine and began busily fashioning a new romper suit out of an old flannelette sheet that she had had stored away. It took a couple of attempts and a bit of tweaking here and there but the end result was surprisingly presentable. So this initial success spurred Fanny on to produce a very elaborate array of clothing for Pants. Clothes for every occasion it seemed and once she thought she had enough to be getting on with she continued to manufacture clothing for Pants in progressively larger sizes, so that he had something to 'grow into'. After all, it wasn't like she could buy clothes for a 2 foot panto horse off the peg, was it? This forward planning by Fanny afforded the other children the chance to dress Pants up in wildly strange outfits, mostly so massively oversized that they did look a little comical. Pants seemed to enjoy this too. He enjoyed being the centre of attention.

It wasn't long before Pants had outgrown the first batch of clothing that Fanny had made.

Horses are measured in 'Hands'. Pantomime horses are no different.

A Hand is 4 inches and measured at the withers (or front shoulders to you and me). A fully grown pantomime horse can grow to about 14 hands which is relatively small in horsey circles. Some of the bigger breeds can reach up to 20 hands or more, whereas a Shetland pony might only be 6 hands. When Pants took his first unsteady steps he was only 3 hands but now in the space of just about 4 weeks had grown to 5 and a half hands! He was growing fast!

Part 2 – 5 ½ Hands

Pants spent a lot of his time careering round the small back garden at Rose Cottage and had become very proficient at it. He could reach quite impressive speeds but with the garden being rather small he would sometimes over cook the corners and end up crashing out and landing in a heap among Fanny's flower beds. Bobby was quick to realize that Pants was going to need a bit more space to stretch his legs as he got older. So, he had a word with Able, whose lambing field backed onto the Blinkett's back garden, to ask if they could steal a bit of it to add to the garden. Able thought it was a great idea. After all, it all belonged to the Endersleigh Estate and he didn't mind losing a little corner of his massive lambing field. In no time at all Able had erected a new fence in the field marking the boundary and had also knocked down the dry stone wall with his tractor and neatly piled the stones at each side of the new, huge garden. It still looked like a sheep field but Bobby could imagine how magnificent it would look with perfectly manicured lawns and perhaps even a cricket pitch! There would be ample room for all the kids to play and Pants could run to his heart's content and expend some of that panto horse energy that he had in abundance.

One day very soon after this, Bobby, Able and Willin were enjoying a swift Ferrets Jockstrap (described as an experimental ale with an earthy but wholesome flavour) in the garden after cutting the grass for the first time when a large black car rumbled to a halt outside the front of the house. Able and Willin immediately recognised it as His Lordships limousine and quickly necked the remainder of their Ferrets Jockstrap and legged it out the back way. Evidently they were not eager to meet with His Lordship. Withers was driving and Hock was sitting beside him, so close that their buttocks were pressed together. Uncomfortably close! His Lordship was seated in the cavernous rear compartment.

Bobby walked round to the front of the house to greet the visitors. Withers and Hock had both exited the vehicle on the driver's side and briskly walked, in their now familiar formation, round the car to the nearside back door. It was one of those backwards opening doors with the handle at the front and hinged at the rear. Withers held open the door for His Lordship to step out. He surveyed the scene, stretching his neck to peek over Bobby's shoulder at the changes that had been made in the garden. Bobby thought he sensed a slight irritation in the peer's demeanour that possibly changes had been made without his consent. It occurred to Bobby also that this was the first time he had met His Lordship in normal attire. He wore a rather tatty looking pair of plus-fours with green socks, brown brogue shoes and a white and blue checked shirt, again a little worn looking and he had a tweed tie tightly knotted at his scrawny neck. His face was unrecognisable without the make-up. That is to say he looked completely different but probably a little more normal than he had the first time they had met. He had a long thin face and a long thin nose. He had removed the flat cap he was wearing revealing his shiny bald head which had only tufts of sparsely spread wispy bum-fluff hair round the sides and back.

Bobby adopted his best posh accent once more.

"Good day to you your Lordship. It is a very pleasant surprise and indeed an honour to greet you on this fine day at our 'umble abode. I must say I hardly recognised you without your bloomers and make-up m'lud and you look just as distinguished in blokes clobber. Na, ha may I assist you Your Grace?" Although it was Bobby's best posh accent, he fooled no-one it really was abysmal and it really grated on His Lordship. Bobby was no fool though he enjoyed the sport. It was a form of bating. He liked to push it to its limit and was always thinking of ever more adventurous titles with which to ridicule the pompous peer.

However, His Lordship began.

"Good day to you Blinkett, I have a task for you to carry out for me. It has come to my attention that you are in printing". His Lordship paused, presumably to see if Bobby would deny the allegation! He didn't and His Lordship continued. "I need posters for the upcoming village pantomime in which, of course, I will be starring as the pantomime dame and my faithful menservants here, Withers and Hock, will as always be playing the ever endearing pantomime horse." He stared intently at Bobby.

"Oh, I fink I can 'andle that your honour. No problem a' all." Bobby had let slip with the posh accent act but thought it a little off that this seeming request of his services came in the form of an order from the odious man.

"But make sure Blinkett that my name is at the top in BIG letter's.......BIG letters Blinkett. Do you understand?" As he was saying this he was also unlatching the gate and pushing past Bobby and making for the door of the house.

"Anyhoo," he said more sedately. "A little birdie tells me that you have a brand new bouncing baby boy." He accentuated 'bouncing'. Perhaps tongues had been wagging! "We've come to pay our respects to your good lady wife and take a look at the newest Blinkett." He snapped his fingers and Hock produced, from behind his back, a rather shoddy bunch of flowers obviously hastily plucked from His Lordships gardens. "So where are they then Blinkett?"

Pants was playing in the play room with his siblings. The other children were piling toys on Pants' back and he was trying to buck and throw them off in one go.

His Lordship, Withers and Hock all pressed their noses up on the glass doors of the play room and looked on in horror.

His Lordship turned to Bobby, his face red with rage.

"So, it is true!...... You know, Blinkett, don't you, that one pantomime horse in any village is quite enough? I trust that you do not have plans for the little blighter above his station!" His Lordship fixed Bobby with an intense, evil stare and was almost nose to nose with him again when Fanny emerged from the kitchen. She had been able to hear what was going on and was none too happy. His Lordship unceremoniously pushed the bunch flowers at her. "Good day to you Mrs Blinkett. Congratulations on your new baby," he snarled.

"Oh, thank you Your Worship. How sweet of you", she opened the door to the playroom and Pants came running at full speed. "Look Pants the nice men brought you some flowers", Fanny held them down to Pants. Pants paused briefly, sniffed the flowers and then grabbed them and tossed them up the air. They all separated and scattered about the floor around the three men's feet and Pants began to dance and buck and frolic in a most frenzied way. He paused on a couple of occasions to pick up one of the flowers in his mouth and then shake it vigorously like a rabid dog. Withers and Hock appeared a little afraid and began to clutch each other and whimper in fear. His Lordship was seething and after a few moments made for the door.

"Shouldn't you be getting on with those posters Blinkett?" he bellowed.

"Straight away Your Landlordship, all over it... all over it ...like a rash...I'll get on to that right now", said Bobby with a wry smile as Withers and Hock scampered to the door of the limousine. His Lordship had arrived before them and was already seated, they closed the door and, in a more orderly fashion, trotted round to the driver seat and reversed in through the front door of the car. His Lordship wound down his window leaned out and shouted, "Remember Blinkett, BIG LETTERS!" and they drove off.

After His Lordship's visit Fanny had very much decided that he and his two 'henchmen' were not to be trusted. There was something peculiar about them. Well sure. That was plain for all to see, but Fanny felt there was more to it than just the zany eccentricity that everyone saw and accepted as normal. She was sure that they were up to no good and she would have to keep a close eye on them.

Bobby set about doing the poster for the pantomime. It would be a fairly straightforward process, but Bobby checked and double checked the dates and venue and all the spelling as he thought it prudent not to upset his Lordship any more. He set out the poster on a sheet of foolscap.

Before decimalisation and Europe foolscap is what they used to call A4 paper. So-called, Bobby thought erroneously, because it was the perfect size for rolling into a cone shape to make a child's 'fools cap' if, in school, they had shown dullard tendencies that day. Bobby shuddered at the thought. Many times had he, as a child, sat in a corner with such a hat on. Grammar had not been his strong point. "But Hey, look at me now", he mused. "Preparing Panto Posters for Pompous Peers," he chuckled, delighted with his alliteration skills.

He finished the poster to his lordship's specifications popped it in a big brown envelope and took it along to Mrs Raunchiman who ran the Post Office. Withers and Hock called in every morning to collect His Lordship's daily paper. They would collect the envelope and pass it on to his Lordship. So he would get it tomorrow morning.

The finished article read:-

VILLAGE PANTOMIME

PUSS IN BOOTS

STARRING

HIS LORDSHIP LORD AVERY CAMPBELL ENDERSLEIGH

as

THE PANTOMIME DAME

and

WITHERS AND HOCK

as

THE PANTOMIME HORSE

and some other people

at

THE VILLAGE HALL

5th 6th 7th and 8th DECEMBER

The next morning, just after breakfast, the phone rang in Rose Cottage. Bobby answered it.

"Endersleigh three three eight", sang Bobby in his trademark phone answering voice.

"BLINKETT, YOU BLITHERING IDIOT!" bellowed His Lordship on the other end of the line. Bobby held the massive antiquated earpiece away from his ear to ease the pain.

"I THOUGHT I TOLD YOU BIG LETTERS!"

"Well me Lud, you do have quite a long name – HIS LORDSHIP LORD AVERY CAMPBELL ENDERSLEIGH," Bobby thought he needed reminding, "It is as big as it can go!"

"WELL BLINKETT IT'S JUST NOT GOOD ENOUGH. I WANT IT BIGGER. BIGGER I SAY!" and once more, "BIGGER!"

"If I make it any bigger it'll be awff the bleedin' page!" Bobby had raised his voice, flabbergasted, but it was too late. His Lordship had slammed the phone down at the other end.

Bobby shook his head and began to think. He was beginning to get a bit annoyed with His Lordships bullying manner.

"HMMMM!" he thought. "Aha!" He had it. With a gleeful smile he got back to the drawing board......literally.

However in keeping with His Lordships wishes Bobby had done His Lordship's name in a huge font but as he had predicted, it didn't all fit on the page. So Bobby, ingeniously, he thought, split the name into three with two separate cards for "HIS LORDSHIP LORD" and the other for "ERSLEIGH" (the remainder of the name which did not fit on the foolscap sheet). The middle part of the name emblazoned across the top of the poster in magnificent big letters as per His Lordship's instructions. Bobby would simply have to pin the first card to the left of the poster and the second to the right. There seemed no need to have it scrutinized by His Lordship as this had been the only complaint with the original draft and Bobby had put this right. So Bobby took his poster across the road to the village notice board and put it up for all to see. He could only find one pin so he taped the two name extension cards to the notice board with clear sticky tape. Bobby stepped back admiring his work. Perfect, he thought.

Later that day his Lordships limousine was burbling along the road through the village with Withers driving, Hock at his side and His Lordship in the back. It cruised past the village hall at a leisurely pace but suddenly came to an abrupt halt a little beyond the village notice board. Then it slowly reversed back until it was adjacent with the notice board.

His Lordship had been on his way to visit his cousin Jasper De Corsey in the neighbouring county to discuss a little business when, out of the corner of his eye he had spotted something on the notice board. After he had called on Withers to stop and waited until he had backed the limousine up, level with it, he wound the window down and stared, squinting over the top of his spectacles at the poster on the board. He couldn't quite make it out so he instructed Withers and Hock to come and open the door. They dutifully obliged. His Lordship stepped out and leaned forward to Bobby's poster on the board holding his reading glasses on his nose with one hand. Withers and Hock were now at his side, also reading the poster intently. Hock had great difficulty as it was not easy to crane his neck up from his stooped position. As they read His Lordship's face became redder, his expression darkened and he ground his teeth in fury.

The poster read:-

VILLAGE PANTOMIME

PUSS IN BOOTS

STARRING

AVERY CAMP BELLEND

as

THE PANTOMIME DAME

and

WITHERS AND HOCK

as

THE PANTOMIME HORSE

and some other people

at

THE VILLAGE HALL

5th 6th 7th and 8th DECEMBER

Withers let out a cackle and an, "Oh dear!" and Hock began to guffaw loudly, snorting like a pig.

His Lordship quickly turned on the pair with a face of thunder, removed his flat cap and began to beat the pair around the ears!

Withers and Hock cowered, with arms raised trying to deflect the blows.

Unfortunately, the sticky tape securing the two cards with the name extensions on had become unstuck in the heat of the glass cabinet of the notice board as it was quite a sunny day. They had fallen off and lay in the bottom of the cabinet unseen. As you can imagine, His Lordship was furious and wasted no time in seeking out Bobby who was sitting in his garden, dressed as Elvis, enjoying a nice cold 'Armpit' and listening to some rockin' Elvis tunes on his gramophone.

Bobby listened to His Lordship's complaint and explained what he thought had gone wrong, apologized profusely and sincerely and assured His Lordship he would rectify the situation immediately. His Lordship breathed a sigh of relief as he drove out of the village believing that he had averted a potentially embarrassing 'faux pas' and that no-one had actually seen the deeply offensive poster.

However, as his limousine burbled on to the edge of the village it passed Canny and Wilney's shed, the flag fluttering gently in the breeze, he thought he heard someone call "Oi! BELLEND!" but he couldn't be sure. In the rear-view-mirror Withers could see Elvis, with some beers under his arm, heading in the direction of the shed, beaming.

Part 3 – 8 Hands

The days stretched into weeks and the weeks into months and Pants continued to grow and learn new skills. The Blinketts had certainly taken to village life and very much enjoyed being part of the close, friendly community. Fanny had met many like-minded new mums through the village toddler group that she attended with Tallulah and Pants and had quite a network of friends within the community. Everyone was always thrilled to meet Pants, he had become quite the local celebrity and everyone adored him. Other mums were keen to arrange play-dates where their kids would come to Rose Cottage and play in the garden with Pants, Tallulah, Mickey and Zoey and the mums would look on enjoying tea and cake and mum-chat with Fanny.

One of Pants' favourite games to play was the bucking bronco game where the other children would pile as many toys as they could onto Pants' back and he would try to buck them all off. Mostly though, Pants enjoyed running and he was now super-fast! He could zip around the garden in no time at all, it was amazing. When the other children arranged races Pants won, every time, hands down. He would reach the finish line and be celebrating his win with a victory dance before most of the other kids had even begun. So they all decided that to make it fairer they would have Pants start from further back until eventually Pants was running twice as far as they were. But it made no difference, the outcome was always the same, Pants would win easily.

One day Willin was in the garden with Bobby watching this spectacle and supping on a Ferret's Crotch. Willin was amazed at the speed of the young Pantomime Horse and remarked to Bobby, "Think he's got a bit of race-horse in him that boy!" Bobby nodded in agreement filled with pride.

Pants' only 'Achilles heel' was his inherent clumsiness! He was, after all, a pantomime horse and pantomime horses were famously clumsy. Their apparent inability to perform simple dance moves or tackle stairs was legendary. It was normal for a pantomime horse to be gangly and awkward. Pants was no exception, although, HE could run like the wind, a skill that would come to serve him well in the future.

As if to prove my clumsiness point in a most opportune manner, Bobby had picked up second hand bikes each for Zoey and Mickey. Tallulah was still too small for a proper bike and anyway had now inherited Mickey's wee trike. Mickey still needed stabilizers but Zoey could just about manage ok if her dad helped her off with a push. Bobby, like every dad at this very important moment in a child's life, was understandably nervous and keen not for Zoey to fall off and hurt herself so ran alongside until he was sure that she was stable and steady. It wasn't long before she was scooting up and down the pavement with ease.

Pants decide that this was very much a skill that was achievable for him. He was confident of mastering it with minimum fuss!

Zoey could see that he was keen to try so offered her bicycle to him to have a go.

First Pants tried to manoeuvre his bottom onto the saddle and then throw his front legs over the handle bars but he always ended up in a heap. Bobby even tried to hold the bike for him but after much shouting and screaming Bobby would end up in a heap with him. Next he tried pedalling with his front legs and just running behind with his back legs. This was a little more successful but wasn't really riding a bike. He gave up at this point. Obviously cycling was not for him.

But Bobby had an idea.

The next day, after work, Bobby arrived home with a small tandem – A bike for two.

Pants jumped on. Front legs pedalling. Back legs pedalling. Hey presto! Easy as pie! Pants was off.

After that, on Sunday afternoons the Blinketts were often seen out cycling along the Endersleigh road. Bobby on his 1930's bike with the funny looking handlebars that pointed backwards, Fanny's had a lovely basket on the front and a child seat at the back for Tallulah. Zoey's bike was pink and very swanky and Mickey would be rattling away at the back with tassels hanging from his handlebars and rocking from side to side on maladjusted stabilizers. Pants could go quite fast on his tandem but was prone to falling off regularly as he had trouble steering the thing but it did not dishearten him at all. He never seemed to hurt himself and, as I said, Pants expected the odd comedy tumble, it was in his DNA.

It was now almost 2 years since the Blinketts had made the move to Endersleigh and the arrival of Pants which had so transformed their lives. Bobby was enjoying his job greatly and had got the promotion that he had so much wanted. He was now heading his team within the humour department. He liked nothing more than to sneak into conversation some of the new jokes he was trying out on his new line of greetings cards in an effort to gauge the hilarity of them. He saw it as market research! Most were not that funny. Like, - What do you call a man with a car on his head? …..Jack.

Or, - What do you call a man with a bush on his head? .....
Russell.

Or, - Seagull? ....Cliff. You get my point. Not that funny.
However, he did have a whole array of funny elephant jokes which
were hilarious and the children wanted to hear them over and over
again, however it would be irresponsible of me to repeat them here
for fear of splitting the readers' sides!

Fanny was now a member of the pantomime group and had been
in two pantomimes. They called themselves, rather grandly Fanny
thought for a small village panto group, 'The Endersleigh Players'.
Fanny had impressed them all immensely in the first year even
though she was just trusted with only a few smaller roles and so, in
the second year, had been cast as the principal boy - effectively the
lead role and "Had", said the critics in the Endersleigh Evening
Gazette, "lifted the Endersleigh Panto to new heights." Fanny was
thrilled.

All the players had learned to put up with the constant
complaining, the demands and the diva like behaviour of His
Lordship and the sheer incompetence of Withers and Hock. Fanny
had been shocked at how terrible the trio were and how badly they
treated all the other players which only made her disdain towards
them grow all the more, but like everyone else in the village, she
learned to just carry on regardless and tolerate them.

Pants would come along to rehearsals with Fanny and sit quietly
on the mats on the floor at the front of the stage with his chin resting
on the stage looking up at Fanny and the other cast members going
over their lines. Children were usually not allowed to come to
rehearsals as it was thought that it would ruin the surprise for many
as the children would be discussing the panto at school before the
actual performances. It would be best to keep it, as much as possible,
a secret. Fanny felt, though, that this rule could be relaxed for Pants
as, after all, he WAS a pantomime horse and as we know pantomime
horses don't talk......much. Fanny was convinced in her mind that
Pants would, as soon as he was old enough, want to audition for the
part of pantomime horse and everything would be as it was intended
to be. She was merely preparing him for the inevitable.

Pants, however, was in two minds. Sure, he would like to at some point appear in a panto or two, but there were also a lot of other things that he wanted to do. He wanted to learn new stuff, go to new places, meet new people and experience life.

He was still young though and had a lot to learn.

Chapter 7

Pants Down

Part 1 – 10 Hands

Pants' first day at school had arrived and Fanny, now an expert with the sewing machine had made him a very smart school uniform. (The Marks and Spark's 'Back to school' range didn't include anything in pantomime horse sizes.) It consisted of two pairs of grey trousers and a very broad blue blazer with the Endersleigh school 'Coat of Arms' on the breast pocket. The blazer stretched from his withers to his hocks and Fanny had made a matching blue school cap out of the left-over material.

Pants was excited to be going to school, he knew all the children and they all knew him. The only thing he was unsure about and a little afraid of, if the truth be known, were the teachers. There were only two teachers in the whole school as there were only 31 children, including Pants. They were Mr Harvey the head and Miss Pettigrew. Mr Harvey was a serious sort of chap and had a fearsome reputation. He carried his belt, or 'tawse', over his shoulder under his tweed jacket as if it was a gun in a holster like in the Dirty Harry films.

The tawse, pronounced 'toss', was a leather strap specially made for punishing naughty children. It was about 30 inches long and separated into three strands at the receiving end to maximise the recipient's pain. Some of the older kids had actually witnessed him split a bench with it. He wasn't shy of using it either but only if you were really bad.

Miss Pettigrew, on the other hand, was very mild in comparison, some twenty years older than Mr Harvey and very slight. She did not possess a tawse but if the conditions were met she would call in Mr Harvey to administer 'justice'. Kind of like a contract killing of sorts.

Miss Pettigrew had a tendency to sometimes fall asleep in the classroom as she was getting on a bit. One day one of the older children, a big bruiser of a lad called Robin Redpath, the school bully, who was known as Ripper, changed the clock forward two hours when Miss Pettigrew had fallen asleep and when the break-time bell went and Miss Pettigrew was woken she thought it was home time and sent all the kids in her class home. Mr Harvey went ballistic and the next day grilled all the children in Miss Pettigrew's class individually. He was very adept at getting to the truth in a situation such as this. At least three of the children spilled the beans and dobbed in Ripper who subsequently received 'six of the best' from Mr Harvey. Ripper was sure he heard Mr Harvey say, under his breath, just before his first delivery "Go ahead punk, make my day." Ripper received a lovely set of stinging red stripes on his hands and returned to his classroom, his eyes moist. He had let it be known to the other kids that if he found out who had dobbed him in, then he was going to give them 'a right doing'. Everyone remained tight-lipped though and Ripper soon forgot about his crusade and things returned to normal.

All the children, including Pants, looked forward to play-times and the games they played were varied. Pants tried his hand at most.

Sometimes they played football. Pants watched with interest before joining in and quickly got into a right fankle. He was fine when he was running off the ball but as soon as he got the ball at his feet he couldn't decide which foot to kick it with. Panic would set in and he would end up tripping himself up and landing in a heap. The other kids suggested he try being in goals, just to get him out of the way really, and this proved to be his forte. He would just stand side-on in the goal mouth and straight away he had an advantage over the other children as his 'side' took up most of the goals. If the opposition strikers came near his goal he would run out in a sideways manner, much like a crab, 'closing down the angle' making it impossible for the opposing team to score, and if they dallied too long Pants would flatten the poor unfortunates.

Another game played frequently, mostly by the girls, was hopscotch where you had to hop and jump with one or two feet into squares marked on the ground in chalk. Pantomime horses are not natural hoppers and Pants found this particular activity nigh on impossible. On Pants' first to fifth attempts the end result was always the same, an untidy mess somewhere near the beginning. Hopscotch was not for him.

Pants tried rounders. It looked fairly simple! Mr Harvey insisted that they play with a tennis ball as it was safer - and just as well really. When batting, Pants held the bat in his mouth but when the ball was tossed in his direction he swung, missed completely and the ball smacked him squarely on the face every time. So they all agreed that Mickey could bat for Pants and Pants would just have to run round the bases. This he could do. Every time Mickey struck the ball Pants set off at breakneck speed round the bases and had usually returned to home-base before the ball had hit the ground! He was just a blur. Zip. Zip. Zip.

Generally, they all agreed, there were some games Pants could play but mostly he was just Pants...... It was meant as a joke but it did make Pants feel a little sad.

Between the months of July and December every year Fanny would get busy with panto stuff. Since joining the panto group she had acquired many additional duties.

There was first the process of sitting down with the other Endersleigh Players to decide which pantomime they were going to perform. This was sometimes a very heated affair as some of the players had definite favourites and some had pantomimes they hated.

Then there was the business of writing the script. Fanny hadn't done any script writing before but found it was easier than she had at first thought it might be as she was familiar with the structure of a good panto and the others helped to add in some of the local interest points like, - Farmer Sharp crashing his tractor into a ditch or Mrs Raunchiman of the Post Office being awarded an M.B.E. for services to the local community for her charity work, - that kind of thing.

Then there were the auditions where competition was keen, although they tried to ensure that everyone who turned up got a role to play. No-one would be sent home with nothing. Of course the parts of the pantomime dame and the pantomime horse were always taken by His Lordship, Withers and Hock. Everyone just accepted it and worked round it.

Then there was the small matter of all the costumes. Fanny had this responsibility too as the other members had come to learn of her skill with a sewing machine. Her task was made slightly easier because His Lordship insisted on producing his own costumes. He had a tailor friend from Savile Row in London who would come and measure his Lordship up and produce a different, very elaborate and expensive made-to-order dress for every scene that His Lordship was in. He also had a very impressive selection of wigs in every conceivable colour. Blonde, black, pink and green being just a few. Some straight, some curly, some frizzy and some in elaborate bouffant beehive styles. His Lordship insisted on having his own dressing room to accommodate all his costumes, and everyone else shared the other one.

But still Fanny had to produce all the costumes for everyone else. This would take up most of her free evenings between August and November until they were all ready.

As the December performance dates grew closer everyone would get more nervous and start to panic about learning their lines in time. Everyone, that is, except His Lordship. He never learned his lines properly and often the rehearsal would stall as he would painfully slowly start to recall his forgotten line until Withers and Hock would trot up beside him and offer him his script.

"I don't need my script", he shouted on one occasion. "I know my lines. Just a bit rusty, that's all", and as nothing else was coming to mind he just threw in a random, "Tickety-Boo!" and walked off stage leaving Fanny and the other producers shaking their heads in disbelief.

Withers and Hock thankfully had no lines to learn but they found even the simplest stage direction a challenge. They would be asked to come on stage at the end of a particular song but instead would be found, in full panto horse costume, in a dark corner of the back stage area oblivious to the fact that their presence was required on stage. Fanny appointed one of the young stage hands to nurse-maid them.

The performances were generally met with indifference. There seemed to be a general apathy among the community with regard to the pantomime. In its heyday, the pantomime would run for eight nights over two weekends and they would play to a packed house every night. Sometimes they would throw in matinee performances too, but due to dwindling numbers this was reduced to just 4 performances over one weekend, Thursday to Saturday and even then they had difficulty filling the hall. Many attended purely because they were employees of His Lordship and were expected to attend or risk losing their Christmas bonus (which was usually just a pheasant or a duck). Some attended with the kids purely because Mum or Dad had a small part in it or were helping backstage. Some parents treated it like an affordable child-care scheme and dropped the kids off and headed out to the pub and picked the kids up on the way when the panto had ended. This was unusual and considered very undesirable behaviour. Some attended because they hadn't been before and were hoping for an evening of top-notch entertainment only to be sorely disappointed.

It wasn't that the panto's were bad. It was that His Lordship, Withers and Hock were absolutely dire and no amount of fancy jiggery-pokery from the other Endersleigh Players could conceal the fact! Everyone tried their best and there were some sterling individual performances which were greatly received by the pantomime diehards and close family members but the reluctant attendees remained ominously silent throughout.

Fanny would ensure that every year the Blinketts would get front row seats on at least two of the performance nights and the kids would be crouched on the mats at the front with any other of the kids in attendance. Pants would rest his chin on the stage and watch lacklustre performance after lacklustre performance and sometimes feel the embarrassment of the poor unfortunate on the stage. Pants paid particular attention to the pantomime horse of course. This was truly embarrassing too at times and Pants wondered how this pantomime horse was just so inept at even the most basic and instinctive pantomime horse moves, until he realised it was Withers and Hock and it all made sense to him. They were not exactly glowing role models for aspiring young pantomime horses and Pants desire to be part of this embarrassing fiasco diminished over time.

Fanny's ardour was not dampened though and her desire remained for Pants to mature into the finest Pantomime horse there was and for him to join her in the Endersleigh Players and "MAKE ENDERSLEIGH GREAT AGAIN." (She had not forgotten her humble Trump roots) producing the best Pantomimes for miles around. Fanny would often daydream:-

Pants would be performing to rapturous applause and laughter in a packed Endersleigh Hall with all the local dignitaries and press in attendance. Flowers being thrown at Pants' feet and calls of "Encore" ringing out as Pants takes the final curtain and then the reporters and fans going crazy backstage for a glimpse of the magnificent Pants Blinkett…….

Fanny was jolted back to reality as everyone backstage was whispering loudly over a hushed audience, "Does anyone know where Withers and Hock are…..they're supposed to be on!"
"They're in my dressing room having a poo," boomed out His Lordships voice in the darkness. "Shouldn't be long. Tickety-boo!"

Hock had insisted to Withers that he really, really needed to go.
"But, my good fellow, we are due on the stage in a matter of minutes, we may miss our cue", said Withers.
"Vee must get to zee sheizer immediately Vithers, I em touching cloff beck here!" said Hock, his thick German accent sounded rather panicky although muffled.
There was a toilet cubicle in His Lordships dressing room and they hastily made their way there and burst in on his Lordship who was touching up his lippy.
"What the…..?"
"An emergency Your Lordship. Hock needs to go Sir".
"Bloody hell Withers, can't he just piss in a bucket?"
"It's a number two, Sir", said Withers with a slight amount of disgust evident in his tone.
The back end of the pantomime horse suddenly wheeled round, to the front ends surprise, and was reversing at speed towards the

cubicle in the corner of the dressing room and there wasn't a damned thing that Withers could do about it.

His Lordship, sensing what was about to transpire made a hasty exit and left the pair to their own devices.

Hock had dropped his pantomime horse trousers and had reached the relative safety of the cubicle and seated himself in the nick of time. Meantime the front end of the pantomime horse was biting the door surround in an attempt not to be dragged any further into the now foul smelling enclosure.

The door of the dressing room opened as the young back-stage boy called in.

"Last call for the pantomime horse. You're on in......", his mouth fell open as he tried to make sense of the scene that confronted him. The pantomime horse was squatting in the lavatory with its front half apparently chewing on the door surround woodwork as great voluminous farting explosions emanated from the depths of the tiny convenience.

The hall lights went up and Fanny made the announcement, "Ladies and Gentlemen, there will be a short intermission while the pantomime horse takes a poo. Juice and biscuits can be bought at the back of the hall." Fanny could not hide her embarrassment. This was indeed a new low! Something had to be done about Withers and Hock.

Pants hung his head with feelings of shame and nausea as the image of Withers and Hock pooing in His Lordships dressing-room was etched on his memory forever.

Cricket was another of Bobby's great loves. It wasn't widely played in Scotland and the rules, in truth, were a mystery to most Scotsmen. Bobby endeavoured to enlighten his drinking pals Able, Willin, Canny and Wilney and anyone else who cared to join them on the finer points of the confusing game. He was met with blank stares when he tried to explain some of the intricacies using terms like 'googly' or 'silly mid off' so he set about carefully preparing a pristine cricket pitch in the new expansive back garden of Rose Cottage. He spent hours cutting the grass and rolling the pitch and cutting the grass and rolling the pitch again. Until, one day, it looked like a cricket pitch. It even had the stumps at each end. He invited all the boys round that afternoon and was keen for them all to have a go.

As Bobby expected, no-one had much of a clue about cricket or how to play it and most were not that interested in learning. However, they all had a go at batting and then bowling, some more enthusiastically than others, and Willin refused on account of his condition and Canny was pretty much useless and had the 'co-ordination and manual dexterity of a hard-boiled egg' Bobby had noted. Wilney wouldn't even try and just supped his Ferret's Armpit and watched. However the children, Zoey, Mickey, Tallulah and Pants were all itching to have a go. So, Bobby decided after a short period of practice that they would divide into two teams, the children included, and have a match. Able was appointed team captain of the opposing side as he was probably the most promising prospect of the whole sorry bunch. In all they had ten willing participants and they split into two teams of five. Pants and Tallulah were on Bobby's team.

The match started with Able's team batting. Bobby bowled them all out for no runs in five balls. No-one, but Bobby, enjoyed this much and he very sheepishly apologised for his selfish over exuberance and they started again. This time Bobby's team were batting first and Tallulah was first out as the bat was a little too heavy for her, she could hardly lift it. Then it was Pants' turn.

"Right then my boy," said Bobby, who evidently thought it necessary to give Pants a little pep-talk. "Keep your eye on the ball and step in to it son."

Pants held the bat in his mouth. He was aware that rounders had proved to be a bit of a challenge but was confident that cricket would turn out to be his thing. Able produce an immaculate delivery and Pants swung the bat at the approaching ball. Whoosh! He missed it completely and it bounced off his nose causing him to release the bat, sending it sailing in a perfect arc to the other end of the pitch where 'Plink'. The sound of willow on bone as the bat made contact with Bobby's head!

"Ouch!" he screamed and to add insult to injury the ball had bounced off Pants' nose and wiped out the stumps.

"Owzat!" cried Able with his arms aloft in triumph.

Pants skulked off dejectedly. Bobby rubbed his head vigorously. Only he and Pants were not able to see the funny side of this unfortunate incident.

"It's fine Pants, my boy. Don't worry about it. You'll soon get the hang of it. You just need to keep your eye on the ball and concentrate."

Pants next opportunity to shine came when it was his turn to bowl. Bobby's team were letting him down badly and there were only a few points in it. This delivery was crucial and Bobby, it seemed, was not a good loser. (He called it a competitive spirit.) All was depending on Pants.

Bobby stepped in for another pep-talk. "Right then Pants, nice long strides – release early and a nice big follow through. Got it? This is it Pants. Goo on my son!"

Pants was confident that he could pull this off and Bobby would be so proud and so pleased when Pants successfully bowled out Able at the other end. He held the ball in his mouth and walked back to line up a huge run-up. He rubbed the ball into the front of his trousers. He didn't know why, but he had seen Bobby doing it and it seemed to work for him. He began his run-up, reaching a truly impressive speed just before the release point where he tripped up and went careering and tumbling down the pitch, first taking out the stumps at his end and still having the momentum to wipe out the wicket, batsman and wicket keeper at the other end. It was carnage. Bobby's team lost by default and Bobby was livid. In the heat of the moment he had said it was 'an affront to his English cricketing heritage' but he soon calmed down and tried to adopt the persona of a magnanimous loser and insisted to Pants that it was fine - not to worry - it wasn't his fault.

But Pants was distraught, he hung up his pads, bat and two boxes for good. Cricket was not his thing either, but worst of all, he had let Bobby down.

Part 2 – 12 ½ Hands

Pants had now matured into a very handsome pantomime horse and stood an impressive 12 and a half hands tall. He was pretty much done growing and was quite satisfied with his stature. He would sometimes catch sight of his reflection in the big window onto the garden and stand and posture, imagining himself as perhaps a household cavalry horse or a rodeo trick pony or an actor in the movies playing alongside the likes of John Wayne or James Stewart. He wasn't sure yet what he wanted to do when he 'grew up'. He was sure of one thing though and that was that it was a big old world out there and he wanted to sample some of it for himself.

Although he was generally happy most of the time, he sometimes became sad and felt down because he always seemed to be messing up and breaking things or disappointing Bobby. He knew though that Fanny had never been disappointed in him and she only wanted one thing for him. For him to be in the Endersleigh pantomime. He felt that her disappointment was not far away.

Sports day was always a bit of challenge for Pants but he always liked to have a go at everything and this year was no different. He was entered into all the races.

First there was the 'Egg and Spoon race'. Pants held the spoon between his teeth, like a flamenco dancer would a rose. Pantomime horses have a natural ability to hold their heads very still and steady regardless of outside interference. This is deemed a necessary trait, and second nature to most pantomime horses, as it maximises the comedy effect of catastrophic tumbles if they retain all the liquid contents within a vessel clutched in their mouths during slapstick comedy routines. This means during all kinds of erratic running and tumbling and horse play making 'egg and spoon' races a formality for Pants and he would always win with ease.

Then there was the 'Wheelbarrow race'. He needed Mickey's assistance for this one. Mickey held Pants' back legs aloft but Pants could run just as fast on just his front legs and Mickey barely managed to keep up. They won this easily too.

Then there was the 'Three legged race'. Simple! Mickey tied Pants' back legs together, which, in truth was only a minor inconvenience to Pants and he won this with ease too.

At the finishing line the judges were waiting to pin on the appropriate colour of medal to the winners, runners-up and third placed competitors. Ripper, who had turned into a mountain of a boy and now towered above everyone in the school including Dirty Harvey, as the head had come to be known, was getting mightily miffed as he had not won a race yet while Pants was beginning to resemble a decorated war veteran with all his gold gongs. All the while Ripper, who was a very competitive sort, was getting madder and madder. It didn't help that Pants was show-boating a little during the final stages of the sprint as he was so far ahead he could afford the time to walk over the line walking only on his front feet with his back feet dangling in the air.

Bobby, who had come to the Sports Day dressed as Elvis, was watching with Able and Willin. They had all known that Pants had a turn of speed about him in the past but they hadn't realised that since the young pantomime horse had grown big that he was actually as fast as this. This was incredible! They all watched in awe, with mouths agape, as Pants won race after race and simultaneously began to daydream……..

Pants is a racehorse - romping home to victory ahead of a field of actual real racehorses and Bobby, Able and Willin are all cheering ecstatically at the finish line waving wads and wads of cash, Pants standing atop a grand podium wearing the winners garland of roses while Bobby, Able and Willin crack open a huge Magnum of Champagne, spraying each other and the exuberant crowd with its contents…….

The trio of daydreamers were then rudely jolted back to reality as young Mickey cracked open a very fizzy bottle of pop and accidentally sprayed the contents into their faces.

The last race of the day was the 'Obstacle race', where there were a series of barriers to jump over, some poles to weave in and out of and a final horizontal pole near the finish line to limbo under.

Zoey, Mickey and Tallulah were watching from the side as all their races were now over and all watched in quiet admiration as Pants sailed majestically over the jumps and weaved effortlessly in and out of the poles and they all simultaneously began to daydream……

Pants is a show jumper at the Horse of the Year Show with the ever popular Harvey Smith on his back. They sail effortlessly over massive jumps and end the course to rapturous applause as they smash the course record and Harvey Smith salutes the Royal Box with his trademark 'V' sign………

The three were woken from their over vivid imaginings as Pants tripped over the limbo bar as he realised a little too late that it was actually not a jump and he tumbled to an untidy halt just short of the finish line and Ripper romped home to a seemingly unlikely victory and burst into floods of tears as he received his first gold medal of the day and the traditional obstacle race crown and sceptre. Zoey, Mickey and Tallulah thought it reminiscent of the Miss World beauty contest where the winning lady is crowned 'Miss World', invariably in floods of tears also.

Ripper was not one to harbour a grudge but on this occasion he harboured a grudge! There were two reasons really that brought him to the conclusion that beating up Pants was the only dignified course of action open to the school bully. Number 1 was that Pants had pretty much won every race at the sports day and this was a huge affront to Ripper and number 2 was that by Pants not winning the obstacle race he was the reason for Ripper's very public display of pent up emotion being released and hence him looking like a complete lemon.

As was normal in these situations the school bully had at least two apprentice bullies and Ripper was no exception. He had Cammy Biggar and Cammy Weir who were, as you'd expect, called Big Cammy and Wee Cammy. Frustratingly, though, Big Cammy was wee, wee'er than Wee Cammy and Wee Cammy was bigger than Big Cammy but still wee'er than Ripper.

Ripper had Big Cammy and Wee Cammy primed that after school on this particular day they were going to 'get' Pants and teach him a lesson! On this particular day though, Pants was late out of school for some reason and only Zoey waited for him to walk the relatively short distance home. Zoey and Pants were sauntering up the middle of the tree lined road in a very picturesque part of the village past the church, Zoey chatting excitedly about girly things that really didn't interest Pants in the slightest, when all of a sudden Ripper and Big and Wee Cammy appeared from behind a tree on their bikes.

"Right ya wee bampot!" said Ripper. "Ah'm gonnae gie you a right good kickin'! 'moan boys let's get 'um."

Although Zoey was a bit of a fighter herself and a very protective big sister, she knew she had next to no chance of seeing off these three. She knew also that of 'fight' or 'flight', 'flight' was the only smart option here.

"Run Pants! Run!" she shouted in a strangely southern fried chicken kind of accent.

Pants did as he was bid and took off at speed in the direction that they had just come from as his path home was blocked by the three bullies. They set off in hot pursuit with Zoey calling after them, "Run Pants! Run! Don't let them catch you Pants!"

Zoey felt relatively satisfied that Pants could easily outrun the three even if they were on bikes, as did Pants and he settled into a comfortable gallop along the tree lined route with Ripper and Co. a safe distance behind. Pants knew they would tire long before he did.

As Pants rounded a bend just past the school he caught sight of a truly wondrous sight. Not particularly wondrous to you and I perhaps but it certainly caused Pants' ears to prick up and his gait to slow ever so slightly. Through the passing trees in a field off to his right there were two horses, a mare and a stallion, fondly caressing each other's necks and a little way off to their side was a young foal. Pants was transfixed and began to daydream:-

As the trees flicker past to Pants right in an instant the two horses change to two pantomime horses, a male and a female, gently caressing each other's necks in a mutual nuzzle and the foal had become a little baby pantomime horse..........

66

As his gallop slowed and Pants craned his neck to view the scene now passing to his rear his directional control was sadly lost and his innate clumsiness returned and BANG!

Pants had collided with a big old oak tree and ended up lying in a heap at the base. The bullies were soon upon him and began laying into him with exuberant vigour and violence.

Pants didn't really feel pain. Part of his pantomime horse make-up. He knew they would soon tire of beating him and all the while his mind was filled with the vision of the loving pantomime horse family that he had fleetingly imagined. Pants wondered if he could ever be that happy as Ripper bounced another punch off his nose.

Pants soon got his chance to see the horse family again that he had seen during his bungled escape from the three bullies. Zoey and Mickey had arranged for Pants to visit Charlotte Bone-China's riding stables at the other end of Endersleigh village. They had felt that now was the ideal time to put into action their plan for Pants to become a world class show jumper! Charlotte was very well spoken, some might say extremely posh, on account of her having royal connections. She was confident and very loud despite her diminutive stature and she was very knowledgeable about all things horsey! Who better to advise them all on a sure-fire course of action that would lead to ultimate show jumping success, glory, fame and riches etc, etc….

Charlotte began by inspecting Pants very thoroughly! She looked in his mouth forcing his jaws apart quite forcefully and plinked his teeth with her fingernail.

"Hmmmm!" she said. Then she lifted each of his feet in turn and inspected the soles prodding them with her finger. She lifted his tail and inspected underneath. Pants' eyes widened as he feared the worst but it didn't happen. Charlotte finally gave her opinion on Pants' general condition.

"I have seen better", she said loudly. Pants felt only slightly insulted but agreed to continue.

Charlotte mounted her huge mare that was already tacked up and waiting. She then took the mare on a slow majestic canter round the riding school arena which was set up with many massive jumps. After a short warm-up Charlotte and the mare began to sail effortlessly over all the jumps in sequence and after the last rode over to Zoey, Mickey and Pants and leapt from the saddle landing neatly on her feet beside them. She addressed Pants directly.

"Right then! That's how it should be done. Now it's your turn. Awf you go."

There must've been some kind of breakdown in communications as Pants was convinced that the intention was for him to copy Charlotte and not the mare. So he duly did.

Pants took a running leap at the mare from the rear and landed sprawled over her saddle, his left legs over her left side and his right legs over her right side. Everyone watching was extremely surprised, none more-so than the mare herself and she took off in an uncontrolled gallop wiping out all of the jumps as she went careering round the ring, Pants clinging on for dear life. Pants amazingly managed to remain on his mount during the whole unfortunate episode and when the horse finally ran out of steam and conceded defeat Pants leapt from his perch and stood beside Charlotte apparently seeking her approval.

"You are a F#@!!#@ idiot and a F#@!!#@ waste of space, you useless F#@!!#@ P#@!*"said Charlotte, which rather shocked the children and Pants. This woman was related to the Queen for goodness sake. "You were supposed to jump the F#@!#@ jumps not mount the F#@!#@ mare you F#@!*#@ buffoon!"

Pants wondered if it was worth having another go or if this particular horse had bolted …both figuratively and literally. He doubted that he would be able to jump the massive jumps anyway and he could see that Zoey and Mickey had been traumatized by his total ineptitude. They all decided to walk away, Zoey and Mickey's dream of show jumping success in tatters for the time being at least and Pants distraught that he had let down Zoey and Mickey. They could hear Charlotte's foul-mouthed tirade of abuse continuing as they rounded the corner and headed for home.

Chapter 8

Jockey Shorts

Fanny could see that Pants wasn't himself, he was much quieter than usual. Zoey and Mickey had told Fanny about the events at Charlotte's and she thought this might be the reason for his depressed mood. Pants didn't even want to go with Bobby, Fanny and the other kids on the Sunday bike ride after lunch and Pants usually couldn't wait to get out on his tandem but he was just down.

Bobby decided he should make an effort to cheer the wee chap up. He knew exactly what he needed to do. Everyone knew that Pants could run like the wind. It was something that he enjoyed doing and something that he excelled at. So Bobby thought that Pants might enjoy a day at the races with the lads. He thought it would do Pants good to get out and experience a bit of excitement outside of Endersleigh and it would give Bobby and the boys the chance to get a sneaky wee bet or two on. Pants eagerly accepted Bobby's invitation and it certainly seemed to pep him up a bit.

Soon race day arrived and Bobby, Able, Willin, Pants and Zoey all piled into the campervan for the drive to Kelso. Bobby had thought that Zoey could keep an eye on Pants while he and the boys were doing a bit of business.

The race track was buzzing. Pants had never seen so many people before, all going this way and that. Some ladies with very fancy hats on and some men in top hat and tails and some dressed less grandly. Bobby and the chaps had made a special effort for their day at the races. Able and Willin were sporting their best tartan trews with matching tartan jackets and ties and each had a carnation in their lapels. Bobby was wearing a very smart Tweed suit with matching cape and deerstalker hat. He was also clamping a pipe in his mouth, though it wasn't lit, and looked very dignified, almost Sherlock Holmes-esque you might say.

The first race of the day had not yet started and Bobby was keen to get into the grandstand so that Pants could get a good view of things. They pushed their way through the mobs of people and eventually reached the grandstand. They seemed to have lost Able and Willin, but they appeared a few moments later with slips of paper having just placed a bet on the first race. There were plenty of empty seats and no sooner had they taken theirs when over the public address system the commentator announced.

"They're off...."

Pants watched in silence as Bobby, Able and Willin gradually built up to a crescendo of frenzied excitement as the horses approached the finish line just in front of the grandstand. It was difficult for Pants to appreciate what was exciting the gents so as he didn't understand the concept of gambling. He did think, though, that the horses were not all that impressive and felt that he could certainly go faster than that.

After another two races Zoey was getting a bit bored and wanted to explore a little and suggested that she took Pants for a pizza. Pants' eyes lit up. He loved pizza. Bobby agreed, but warned Zoey to go straight to the pizza van and come straight back afterwards. It would give Bobby and the chaps the chance to get a few bets on anyway.

Off they skipped to the pizza van and on arrival Zoey ordered a small Hawaiian for Pants and a small pepperoni one for herself. They wolfed them down fairly rapidly and were heading back to the grandstand when Zoey spotted a bin where she could dump their pizza boxes and veered off to the right. Pants, unfortunately, did not spot her sudden direction change and was surprised when he turned back to where Zoey had been but was now not there! He stopped and looked all around but Zoey was nowhere to be seen. With a feeling of rising panic Pants ran in circles, desperately searching for Zoey, bumping into people and becoming a little disoriented. Perhaps, he thought, she had decided to return to the grandstand without him, so Pants decided to make his own way back. How hard could it be?

He pushed through the crowds and spied an opening between two small buildings - an alleyway if you will - and beyond some open ground. Perhaps if he headed for that, away from the crowds, he would be able to see which way to go.

He stood in the open grassy area and surveyed the scene. In the distance he could see the grandstand and….. Yes! The unmistakable form of Bobby in his Sherlock Holmes Tweeds waving in Pants' direction with something white in his hand and at his side the tartan suited Able and Willin doing the same.

Pants assumed they were waving to him and began to canter in their direction hoping that Zoey would be there already.

All of a sudden Pants heard a thunderous thumping noise growing ever louder and approaching from behind and he cast a nervous glance over his shoulder. In a flash, a dozen racehorses and riders ran past him and obscured his view of Bobby and the boys so he quickened his pace and began to ease his way to the front of the galloping horses. On catching sight of Bobby again Pants, once more, quickened his pace and left the pack of bemused jockeys for dead in his wake.

Bobby, Able and Willin had stopped shouting and waving their white thingies and were strangely silent with mouths agape as Pants passed the finish line. He returned to the grandstand where Bobby and the boys were sitting but was met by a horde of photographers all calling for a picture from the enigmatic stranger who had just wiped the floor with the best field of runners that Kelso had to offer. He stood and posed for them, coyly at first, but as his confidence grew then his poses became ever more adventurous. When they had enough Pants turned to re-join his family. He then clumsily tried to climb the hoarding but landed on his nose after falling off in the attempt. He picked himself up and regained his composure and breathed a huge sigh of relief on seeing that Zoey, looking a little flustered having thought she had mislaid Pants, had just returned to the grandstand also.

"Did I miss something Daddy?" asked Zoey, sensing that something was afoot, as Bobby, Able and Willin seemed to be in shock and Pants was attracting a small crowd of admirers.

Mrs Samantha Boscumb-Bagshot, a top trainer of racehorses in the Kelso area, had been watching with interest the events which had just unfolded. She had come to the races with the intention of doing a bit of talent-spotting for upcoming racehorses to add to her stable of already seasoned and accomplished racehorses. She thought Pants would make a very interesting and exciting addition to the team. She introduced herself.

"Hello, Mr Ehh....?"

"Blinkett, Ma'am. Bobby Blinkett." They shook hands. "And this is my boy Pants," said Bobby proudly.

"Well, I have to say I am very impressed with you young man," she said tousling Pants' mane. "I am Sam Boscumb-Bagshot. I run the Bluebairn Stables over at Bairnsley. I'm the head trainer there. I've been on the lookout for new talent and I saw you running earlier. You do have quite a talent there young man. How would you like to come and work for me?" She addressed her question to both Bobby and Pants.

"I have the perfect jockey in mind for you, I am certain you will make a winning partnership. I believe you could both make a lot of money in this game and this would be an opportunity not to miss. What do you say?"

Bobby thought about it for a few minutes and could see no harm in it. Pants would be doing what he loved and making some serious money in the process.

"Well then my boy. What d'ya fink? D'ya wanna go racing?" asked Bobby.

Pants nodded vigorously and Bobby and Sam shook hands on the deal as the photographers circled and snapped away enthusiastically shouting excitedly, "This way Mr Pants, this way Bobby, this way Samantha and big smiles....." FLASH.

The next morning, in Endersleigh Hall, Withers and Hock trotted along the very long corridor to His Lordship's bedroom door. Withers was carrying His Lordship's breakfast tray with his dippy egg and soldiers, tea and morning newspaper. He knocked and entered without waiting for a response and briskly, the pair trotted to the bedside, where His Lordship was already sitting up in bed and Withers laid the tray on his lap.

"I strongly recommend, mi'Lord, that you read the headline this morning," said Withers in his usual pompous tone.

His Lordship picked up the paper and squinting through his reading glasses read aloud.

"'SAMBO SCUMBAG SHOT IN PANTS!' Jolly good show! That ought to teach the damned scoundrel. Bloody marvellous!....But who's Sambo?" said His Lordship.

Withers let out one of his low moaning sighs, rolled his eyes and Hock copied. "No m'Lord, it says 'SAM BOSCUMB BAGSHOT IN PANTS DEAL'. It's the Blinkett boy Sir and Samantha Boscumb-Bagshot is the leading horse trainer in Scotland. It would appear that the lad has some talent and is going to be making serious money!"

"Hmmmm! Can't have that, can we Withers? Unless, of course, some of it is coming our way." He let out an evil laugh but it came out all wrong and he sounded like a girl, it needed work.

And so began Pants' racing career. Sam introduced Pants to his new jockey. I say 'new' but Pants had never had a jockey before and was very excited to meet him. He was an Irishman and his name was Pod which was short for Padraig. And Pod was very, very short. Jockeys are generally on the short side but Pod was half the size of a normal jockey. The perfect size for Pants really.

Pod was also a bit of a nervous type. He was little afraid of heights and it seemed such a long way to fall from the usual 16 and 17 hand giants that he was used to riding, so with Pants, standing at just 12 and a half hands, it seemed like his ideal mount. He didn't say much either. He mainly whimpered in varying degrees depending on the level of his anxiety, however, he did seem to be anxious all the time but more-so when aboard a horse.

"Don't worry Pod," said Sam. "Pants will do all the work, he's a clever lad and you will just be a passenger. You'll be fine."

Pod's riding style was a little unorthodox too, mainly on account of his vertigo and fear of falling to his death. It was not so much a riding style as clinging on for dear life. This little issue was partly resolved with the introduction of some very large safety pins securing pod's jodhpurs to Pants' sheet in four places. There was no way he could fall off now!

In training they would pin Pod in place on Pants' back and when Pants took off at speed Pod's whimpering would gradually intensify to 'petrified scream' as Pants hit top speed and, as Sam said, Pod was merely a passenger with the grace of a ragdoll in the jaws of an angry Rottweiler.

It indeed was a winning partnership though. At the first meeting at Ayr Pants won the first race easily but was declared disqualified on account of being a pantomime horse. Sam appealed and asked the course stewards where, in the rule book, did it state that pantomime horses could not compete? The red face stewards had to concede that there were no provisions in the rules for the exclusion of pantomime horses therefore Pants' win could stand. Pants and Pod went on to win all of their races that day except for one race where Pod was getting bounced about so vigorously that he was catapulted from his jodhpurs and dumped unceremoniously on the course. Although Pants finished in first place he was disqualified for finishing with no jockey inside the jodhpurs and boots still pinned to his back ..... and that was in the rules.

Pod walked across the finish line in his underpants and socks whimpering squeakily, his nerves shot, before being reunited with Pants. He was then lifted up by two big lads, one arm each, and dropped into his riding gear which was still attached to Pants for the next race, this time with the addition of a very tight trouser belt so as to avoid a repeat of the unfortunate incident.

The remainder of the days racing continued without further, significant, incident and the whole group were buoyed with success and popped the cork on a few bottles of bubbly to celebrate their good fortune.

Their winning ways continued.

The next week it was Musselburgh and the pair performed outstandingly, not putting a foot wrong, winning every race by a country mile. They celebrated long into the night popping the cork on a few more bottles of bubbly. Pants had actually started to get a taste for it and on a couple of occasions probably had more than his fair share and suffered an outrageous hangover the next day turning up for early morning training sporting very dark glasses and treading very gingerly indeed so as not to aggravate his pounding head.

After that it was Perth. Pod was slowly becoming accustomed to this unusual partnership and had come to the realisation that Pants would win his races regardless of any input from him. So he decided to take measures to keep himself occupied and take his mind off racing when he was in the saddle in an attempt to safely manage his stress levels. During one race he held his transistor radio to his ear at full volume with his eyes firmly shut throughout the race but was severely rebuked by the other jockeys for unsporting, distracting and disrespectful behaviour. So during the remainder of the day's races he read books. It seemed to work for him and had a calming effect so long as the book was not too scary as he was still quite easily frightened.

On and on they went from race meeting to race meeting, smashing the opposition with ease no matter what the quality of the field. Pants had found his niche.

In the beginning Pants was excited and nervous at every meeting but as the time passed it started to become second nature to him. It was almost like it was so easy he didn't need to try that hard and therefore he lost a little of his focus. After all, what was he trying to achieve? He wasn't interested in becoming rich, and although winning all the time was quite rewarding it was now expected of him and therefore no great surprise, excitement or rush of adrenalin when he did. He was still interested in pleasing Bobby though and it was important to him that Bobby and Fanny were proud of him, he wanted them to be proud for the right reasons and he wasn't sure if this was the right way to do it. It would do for the time being though, he thought, but there were questions that he wanted to be answered.

The money began to roll in. Not only was there their share of the prize money from all the races but there was also all the money made from the bets that Bobby and the boys had made when they could get reasonable odds on 'the rank outsider' pantomime horse. But as word got round about his extraordinary talent the odds shortened considerably and it wasn't worth while betting on Pants 'the dead cert'. And then there were all the sponsorship deals, merchandising, TV and radio advertising deals. Pants was hot property, he was successful, he had money in his pocket but something was troubling him and he realised he was not really, really happy.

One day Pants was out taking a spin in his new E Type Jaguar, driving at speed through country lanes with a beautiful girl in the passenger seat. He was enjoying the thrill of extreme speed with the wind blowing in his mane. He looked at the speedo. It read 100mph. He looked at the girl who was gripping the dashboard nervously and he began to think to himself.

"What have I done to deserve these riches, these pleasures, this carefree lifestyle........this girl?"

Then as the trees flashed past he caught sight of the two horses and foal in the field. His gaze was transfixed. He began to dream.

Again he dreamt of the beautiful female pantomime horse and the baby pantomime horse – but this time the male pantomime horse was himself. He looked up and they made eye contact as the car raced by.

Pants almost lost control of the car as it veered off the road and clipped the bushes and he had to wrestle it back to the road with the girl now screaming in terror with her fingertips deeply embedded in the dashboard.

He looked in the rear view mirror to the field but they were gone.

Chapter 9

Dirty Pants

His Lordship had been getting regular updates from Withers on the seemingly meteoric rise of Pants Blinkett and his incredible success in the racing world. It seemed that the young pantomime horse was undefeatable, and this gave His Lordship an idea. He called on Withers and Hock and instructed them on how to proceed.

Pants was celebrating his victory at the Thirsk Hunt Cup where he and Pod had romped home with a 10 length victory, destroying the course of 21 thoroughbreds. Bobby, the boys and Sam were ebullient and the Champagne was flowing again. Pants was enjoying a glass of bubbly with a beautiful blonde girl, also with glass in hand, her arms clasped round his neck, gently fondling his mane.

Tomorrow was the big race of the season, The Zetland Gold Cup at Redcar, with massive prize money and Pants was determined to do his utmost to win this one and so had decided to only have one glass of bubbly.

No-one noticed the two rather strange looking Hippies, one with a serious stoop, coming in to join the party, besides, a lot of Pants' new friends were Hippies with flower power shirts, colourful trousers, afghan coats, headbands, long hair and dark glasses – that was the look – and Withers and Hock had it off to a tee!

They cautiously sidled to within arm's length of Pants, unnoticed, and no-one saw the 'plop' of the pill going into Pants bubbly glass. They sidled away, unobserved, and waited in the shadows outside.

Pants was having a whale of a time. Life was great all of a sudden. He had not a care in the world and he felt invincible. He was listening to the views of the Hippies when the room started to slowly rotate and the Hippy, called Nigel, who was addressing him sprouted very large whiskers, a black button nose, furry ears from the top of his head and started squeaking like a mouse. Perhaps Pants needed some air.

As he staggered into the garden of the large house Withers and Hock pounced, put a sack over his head and bundled him into their van.

Pants was out cold.

He woke up in the long grass behind a bush at the entrance to Redcar Racecourse. His rump was strangely tender and there was a discarded syringe a little way away in the grass. He couldn't remember much from the night before nor how he had got here but was a little disappointed in himself for apparently exceeding his self imposed limit of one glass of bubbly. He gathered his senses and walked in to the racecourse to try to find his team. His head was clear, he didn't feel hung over but he had the strangest feeling in his back legs. They felt heavy as lead and a little out of control. He hoped this was only going to be temporary, perhaps he had been lying awkwardly.

He found his team but his legs were not improving any as the start of the race grew nearer.

Pod was mounted, pinned on and strapped in. They lined up. The starting gates flew open and they were off! Well everyone except Pants. His front legs had set off at pace but were pulled back by his back legs which had not yet started to run. Eventually they kicked in but Pants had very little control over them.

Pod knew something was wrong when he had reached the end of Chapter 1 of his book and they had not yet crossed the line.

As Pants did finally cross the line the crowds in the grandstand were in fits of laughter, he looked just like a pantomime horse milking the laughs in a comedy silly walk sketch!

Pants was distraught and Bobby, Sam and the boys were furious at Pants. Pod was just relieved to be alive.

As the deflated team trudged back to the Winnebago they bumped into an ebullient, nay effervescent, Lord Avery Campbell Endersleigh with Withers and Hock trotting behind.

"Well young Blinkett," he said grinning from ear to ear. "Looks to me like your racing days are over. It happens you know, young racehorses burning out within the first year of competition. I knew it was just a matter of time before it happened to you. Fortunately for me though, I had a grand on the second favourite and, thanks to you, we got 50 to 1". He beckoned Withers forward and unzipped a bulging holdall to reveal his winnings in cash.... £51,000.

"Oh and don't forget Blinkett. Your rent is due at the end of the week," His Lordship attempted his evil laugh again but it was still well short of the mark!

Sue was very disappointed in Pants and immediately terminated his contract. Pants and Bobby didn't party that night and Pants went to sit with Nigel and his girlfriend Meadow. Nigel's face had returned to normal. They talked all night of deep meaningful things and Pants shared a joint with them. They fired up the bong and Pants shared that too. They spoke of their future plans for an amazing journey to Europe, India and the Far East. A journey of discovery, of enlightenment and to taste life and experience new things and places.

Night after night Pants, Nigel and Meadow would sit and discuss all things supernatural and spiritual and Pants listened with growing excitement. They smoked joints, shared the bong and drank beer till the early hours. Most of the time Pants was either high, wasted or sleeping it off.

Bobby tried to talk sense into him to cease this downward spiral to his own destruction.

"Look lad, don't be down-hearted about Redcar. It was not your fault," said Bobby. "I blame myself. I should never have listened to bloomin' Samantha Boscumb-Bagshott. I should never have got you involved in this racing malarkey. These people are no good son. But you are, and you are loved. Come home to your mother son. She misses you and she wants you home". Bobby was seriously regretting exposing him to the poisonous world of racing and gambling.

But Pants could now see that it was all part of a bigger, spiritual plan for him and his path was clear.

His transformation from successful racehorse to drug addled Hippy was complete. He wore a headband and dark glasses, his sheet was decorated in flowers and he wore an afghan rug.

Pants did come home, albeit very briefly. Fanny tried too to make Pants understand that they loved him and everything was going to be

OK and there was always a place for him in Endersleigh. To no avail. He had only returned to pick up some things and pack a bag.

Later that day Nigel and Meadow pulled up outside Rose Cottage in their VW Beetle decorated in a pink and white flower power design. Pants jumped in to the back, they turned up the radio. It blasted out -

'How many roads must a man walk down,
Before you call him a man,
The answer my friend is blowing in the wind
The answer is blowing in the wind.'

They drove off and headed down the main road to England watched by Fanny and Bobby. Fanny, her eyes filling with tears, wondered when she would see him again but she was certain he would come home in time, he just needed this and she knew it.

Chapter 10

No Pants

Village life went on.

Bobby drove to work every morning in his trusty Campervan. At work he was well regarded and popular among his peers and enjoyed his work. He was very ambitious and put all his energy into doing a good job and impressing his superiors. His enthusiasm and drive had not gone unnoticed and he was soon promoted and given the magnificent title of Head of Humour. He was very proud of the fact that he had now reached the dizzy heights of management and treated himself to a new bowler hat. Fanny had pointed out that the hat looked a little out of place with his long hair and unkempt beard. So rather than embark on a course of extreme grooming he decided to ditch the hat and invest in a pair of corduroy trousers and a jacket with elbow patches. This look, he thought, was much more him. Fanny had to concur.

Fanny continued organising, planning and preparing for pantomime season. When she wasn't writing scripts she was sewing costumes and when she wasn't making props she was designing programmes posters and tickets. Her mind was never far from Pants though, she often thought of him and wondered where he was and what he was doing. At night before she went to bed she would say goodnight to Pants and make sure that the back door was unlocked just in case he should return in the middle of the night.

Zoey, Mickey and Tallulah continued at school in the village although things were much quieter without Pants and not so much fun either. Zoey particularly had a very close bond with Pants as she was the one who looked out for him and protected him from the attentions of the bullies.

Ripper, Big Cammy and Wee Cammy missed Pants too. They had to find someone else to pick on, but they didn't enjoy it half as much as beating up Pants.

Able, Willin, Canny and Wilney went on having their Friday night drinking sessions in the hut and Bobby too was a regular attendee and would only miss it if he was working late but you could be certain that if too much fun was being had then PC Caruthers would be on hand in a flash to close things down.

Some weekends Bobby would organise cricket matches and usually the whole village would attend and it would end up in a huge party going on late into the evening and again would normally attract the unwanted attention of the podgy PC.

At Endersleigh Hall the shady goings on continued with lorries and vans coming and going at all times of the day and night. Withers and Hock drove to the Post Office every morning for His Lordship's morning paper.

The Post Office was the social hub of the village and besides everyone buying their newspapers morning rolls and milk there, they would all come for the social chat with Mrs Raunchiman.

She loved being the centre of attention and the font of all the gossip in Endersleigh and if anyone needed to get news out about an upcoming event or social goings-on then you just had to let Mrs Raunchiman in the Post Office know about it and by the end of the day everyone in the village knew. She was also a very kind and caring person and genuinely cared about the people of the village. She often would ask Fanny, when she was in, about Pants' whereabouts and welfare and would disseminate to all and sundry any information she was given. But invariably Fanny did know much and so over time Mrs Raunchiman asked less and less.

Much of the gossip in the village was regarding livestock that were going missing on a regular basis. Mrs Raunchiman, herself a farmer's wife, was kept updated by Mr Raunchiman who was really quite concerned about sheep and cattle that were going missing from the fields that backed on to the moor. There were rumours of rustlers or strange beasts on the loose and despite much proactive intervention from the farmers they all continued to lose livestock from their fields and were unable to establish the cause. Even with the added involvement of His Lordship and PC Caruthers they were unable to shed any light on the situation. Mrs Raunchiman would pass on to all in the village any losses that she was aware of.

Without fail, every day at precisely 8.05am, Withers and Hock would come tripping into the Post Office for His Lordship's morning paper and any other provisions that they were running low on. It would always be Withers that would address Mrs Raunchiman and she became accustomed to his very pompous manner. She often asked questions of the pair hoping for some juicy titbits from the big house that she could pass on into the community for general gossip but he never gave away anything of interest or value. She had also tried the tactic of addressing her questions directly at the curious Mr Hock who generally responded in single word answers in his thick German accent. Mrs Raunchiman eventually conceded that the pair would remain a mystery. They would return to his Lordship every day, his personal and business details safely intact.

His Lordship Lord Avery Campbell Endersleigh was a very jealous and shallow person. He believed that a person's worth was measured by how much money they had or how much land they owned. He had lots of land having inherited the entire Endersleigh estate and he was working towards becoming a very rich man.

Withers had been a lifelong servant of His Lordship. He arrived at the Endersleigh estate when the young 'Lord in waiting', the heir to the estate, was a teenager.

As a young man Avery was expected to join the army as an officer as was the Endersleigh tradition. A long line of Endersleighs had served King and Country before him and he knew there was no escaping his duty. Withers was conscripted as Avery's valet, as that was the trend then. Gentlemen officers had their valet with them to do all their menial tasks and chores. Withers too regarded this as his duty and carried it out without question.

Avery had not been very highly regarded in the army as a leader of men and when war was declared he was transferred to posts well away from any of the action in order to minimise any damage that he may do, and this suited him fine. His service in the army was mainly spent gambling and goofing off.

One night in 1941 he was involved in a poker game in a prison camp for captured German soldiers. Avery woke in the morning to discover that he had won a German prisoner of war called Heinrich Hock. Most normal people on realising the absurdity of this would have returned the poor unfortunate to his confinement immediately but his Lordship regarded Hock as his legal property and Withers was instructed to keep him on a chain and train him in the art of being an officer's valet. The war lasted for another 4 years during which time Hock was fed and kept out of harm's way and although his treatment may have seemed harsh to others Hock came to be grateful for the protection and furthermore extremely loyal to His Lordship.

At the end of the war Hock was offered his freedom to return to the Fatherland but decided to remain in the employ of His Lordship continuing to learn his craft, however years of being chained behind Withers had left him with a worsening stoop.

The three of them returned to Endersleigh after a fairly uneventful war to find the Estate in a severe state of decline and his father, Lord Rupert Campbell Endersleigh, seriously ill. He died soon after their return and there was not a lot of money left in the pot. Lord Rupert, although he was admired and respected by the people of the village and wider community, was a lousy businessman and the Estate had run into disrepair. He died almost penniless and a young Avery inherited his lands and his debts.

The new lord set about transforming the estate in his endeavours to boost his fortunes. He immediately tripled the rents of all the properties on the estate including the farms. He set up a top notch shooting syndicate where the rich and famous would be taken high up into the Endersleigh hills to shoot grouse and pheasant for huge sums of money. He had many more money making ideas and the will and means to put them into action. The locals were excluded from large swathes of the countryside that had been accessible to them for generations while His Lordship exploited all means possible to swell the coffers of his ever expanding business empire. Large sections of ancient forest with many native and irreplaceable trees were felled and sold for profit. Massive quarries appeared in the hills above Endersleigh and enormous lorries hauled massive blocks of

Endersleigh granite away, morning, noon and night, again for huge profit.

The truth was though that no-one in the village truly new the extent of His Lordships business activities on much of the estate. It was all kept a closely guarded secret and now no-one trusted or respected him or his two sinister menservants.

Life went on in Endersleigh as if Pants had never existed, except for the fact that he had left a huge hole in the lives of all of the Blinketts and they all yearned for his return.....

....

Three long years passed.

....

Pants stood atop Windlestraw Law, the largest of the Endersleigh Hills. In the far distance he could see the beloved hamlet of Endersleigh. The vast forest lay between him and the village but he had made it. He was all but home. After three long years of travelling he had explored several continents and several countries, met countless people, some nice, some not so nice. He had journeyed by all means possible, planes, trains, ships, cars and on foot. He had endured every kind of hardship and he had many stories to tell and was eager to reach his family and make a fresh start. He had nothing to prove any more. His wanderlust was satisfied and he was ready to settle in to village life and just be Pants.

He descended from the hilltop, crossed the moor and continued on into the dark forest for quite a time until he came to a pleasant little clearing and decided to sit and contemplate his impending return. He fell asleep in the warm sunshine.

When he woke he suddenly had the feeling that he was no longer alone. He leapt to his feet and surveyed the scene in front of him to see nothing, but he soon became aware of some movement behind him. He thrust his head between his two ajar front legs looking backwards and, after slowly lifting his tail which had blocked his view somewhat, was confronted by one of the strangest sights he had yet seen in all his travels. There were funny little men standing all around him, all upside down, staring quizzically at him. He spun round to face them. They all wore little pointed hats and very colourful clothes. And there were seven of them.

Seven dwarves!

Chapter 11

Smalls

The seven Dwarves had been living in the forest behind Endersleigh Hall digging in the abandoned coal mines beneath the Endersleigh Estate for many years in search of precious stones which they believed were buried there. They dug all day and into the night, six days a week for years and found nothing. At night they would return to their hut in the deep dark forest behind Endersleigh Hall, the well concealed entrance to the mine being close to the edge of the forest, they had to take care not to be seen by the inhabitants of Endersleigh Hall. After many years of fruitless searching in the abandoned coal mines they decided to extend the excavations and they began to dig new tunnels. Many more years passed as the tunnels grew for miles in every direction under the extensive lands of the Endersleigh Estate. Even after all this time there were no riches to be found. Occasionally though, sink holes caused by the excavations opened up in the ground and sometimes a sheep or a cow would stumble in and fall to its death to the mine below. In fear of being discovered, the dwarves would climb up to the surface and mend the sink hole and after a night of hard toil there would be no trace of the sink hole or the poor doomed animals, much to the befuddlement of the farmers who farmed the land. All of the farmers rented their properties from the Endersleigh Estate and when they reported these, all too regular, losses to His Lordship Lord Avery Campbell-Endersleigh their pleas were met with complete indifference. After all, why should he care if these lazy farmers were not tending to their animals or indeed their stock fences in an appropriate manner! Secretly though he was intrigued as to where these livestock were disappearing to. Were the stupid farmers in fact the victims of sheep and cattle rustlers? His Lordship intended to find out.

So, he decided that he, Withers and Hock would conduct a private investigation of the lands where the livestock had been so mysteriously spirited away. His Lordship suspected foul play. Now, this concern for the financial losses of the farming community were not evidence of a warm caring Landlord looking after the best interests of his tenants but rather the efforts of a cold, heartless, greedy man protecting his investment. After all, if the farmers were experiencing excessive financial losses then they may not be able to pay their rents on rent day and His Lordship loved receiving his rents on rent day. And as we know His Lordship loved money.

After several days of searching the fields for signs of skulduggery, with no success, His Lordship and his two menservants took a break at the edge of the forest and ate a pork pie each and a large bottle of dandelion and burdock fizzy drink between them. However it was too much for the bladders of Withers and Hock who trotted off into the forest to find a suitable tree against which to relieve themselves. It was at this moment that the first of the seven dwarves emerged from the depths of the earth via the semi concealed entrance to the old mines. A minor fracas ensued as, after the two shocked urinating butlers had managed to stem the flow (almost), re-package themselves and do up their flies, they managed to round up and contain the dwarves who were darting in all directions. It really was quite a tricky operation, but after a short time, between them, they were able to contain the errant imps. His Lordship, who had heard the kafuffle kicking off, quickly appeared on the scene and after the noise level had subsided a little (dwarves do tend to scream very loudly) he began to quiz the dwarves re their business in HIS forest. At length, the dwarves recounted their story which in fact spanned several decades in pursuit of untold riches which they believed were buried somewhere beneath the Endersleigh Estate. He informed them that they were trespassing on his land and illegally profiting from HIS abandoned mines! The dwarves were very quick to point out that they had never actually profited from HIS mines in any way as they had to this day found no precious stones there, just the occasional sheep or cow from above. They explained to His Lordship about the unfortunate sink hole incidents and the fate of the animals who strayed into them. This was indeed wholly unintentional and they were very sorry! However, none of the animals went to waste or died in vain as the dwarves made the most succulent pies from the meat of the unfortunate beasts as this was the most sensible way of dealing with what was in fact a tragic accident. His Lordship dismissed their apology and, not one to miss an opportunity, made the dwarves a surprising offer! Withers and Hock were really very surprised and disappointed that His Lordship had not immediately evicted the 7 imposters.

"I am prepared to let you remain in your house in the forest if you agree to work for me. But you must remain within the forest and never leave and you must under no circumstances tell anyone of your business here". The dwarves had little choice and agreed reluctantly even though they were still not fully aware of the dastardly plan that His Lordship had in mind.

By now it was clear to his Lordship that the dwarves' sink holes were the cause of the farmers' misfortunes and in the time it took the babbling dwarves to divulge their life stories to the three of them, His Lordship had already devised a sneaky, wicked plot to make himself a lot of money. The dwarves were all marched off to their hut in the depths of the forest under the supervision of Withers, Hock and His Lordship. The dwarves were instructed not to leave the hut until they received further instructions from His Lordship. After the dwarves were all inside Withers mustered the courage to enquire of his master. "Would it be prudent to enquire of His Lordship what his plan may entail?"

"We, my good fellow, are going in to the PIE business!"

This is how it would work. The dwarves would set to work opening up random sink holes and wait for the cattle or sheep to drop in. Once they had enough to be getting on with the dwarves would climb up, as they had done in the past, and make good the sink holes. Then the dwarves who, by their own admissions, were all excellent chefs would butcher the beasts and make lots and lots of the aforementioned succulent pies. On an agreed day the pies would be transported to the large supermarket chain Laldey's which, incidentally, was owned by His Lordships second cousin Jasper De Corsey. Jasper would be sure to pay a very reasonable price for cousin Avery's succulent pies. It really was the perfect plan! Because for no outlay whatsoever His Lordship would make an absolute killing (the author apologises for this unintentional pun).

Over the ensuing few weeks the dastardly trio wasted no time in setting in motion the wheels of the new venture and the dwarves began their forced employment under the close supervision of His Lordship's staff. It proved to be a very successful plan and as time passed the operation grew larger and more livestock were drained from larger and more numerous sink holes. More pies were produced and sold to Laldey's Supermarkets and His Lordship's bank balance swelled with the increased profit of the illicit venture. Of course the poor farmers were at their wits end. No sooner would they buy in new stock and they would fatten them up than they would disappear from the face of the earth. No trace!

Farmers in other neighbouring counties all drove fancy 4 by 4's but the farmers of the Endersleigh Estate all drove crappy old tractors as they were so poor as a result of their unfortunate predicament with the unexplained and intriguing losses. His Lordship was no fool though. He was well aware that there would be a limit to the numbers that he could siphon off before the farmers threw in the towel completely, and that would mean no rent and no supply of meat for his pie industry. He really was a nasty piece of work.

Try as they might, the farmers could never catch the rustlers in the act, nor come up with any other reasonable explanation as to the fate of their missing beasts. Some of the farmers even slept in their clapped out tractors at the gates of the fields only to wake in the morning to find that 2 or 3 animals had vanished! Rumours began to spread of a massive beast that lived in the forest and came out at night and devoured sheep and cattle whole. "The Beast of Endersleigh" they called it.

His Lordship, fearful of a mob descending upon his pie enterprise in the forest, quickly dispelled the rumours by telling the farmers that he had recently inspected the forest and there were no beasts of any sort within as he would not tolerate trespassing. Anyone caught trespassing in the forest was likely to be shot by His Lordship's eager gamekeepers. So the farmers put away their pitchforks and burning torches for the time being and returned to their farms and just hoped that things would get better.

Chapter 12

Underpants

Pants lay in the grass looking up at the seven faces all looking back at him. He was contemplating his next move. Should he make a run for it? Should he just wait and see which way this thing went? They might just leave him be. He slowly rose to his feet and was seriously contemplating the former of the two options when he became aware of something round his neck. There was a rope around his neck and as he stood two of the dwarves took up the slack and pulled on the rope. On feeling the restriction, Pants began to back away in panic and two other dwarves grabbed the rope and helped to pull him back. Pants' eyes widened with fear and he began to pull back frantically and buck and twist in a futile attempt to free himself of his bonds.

"Whoa! Whoa!" they all shouted, "Calm down horsey were not going to hurt you."

Pants stopped and stood still breathing heavily and snorting with flared nostrils. He blew hard and all the dwarves were sprayed in bucket-loads of horse snot, which is not very pleasant, and all but one let go of the rope and began wiping the gooey muck off themselves in disgust.

"That is absolutely mingin'", said one.

"Gads!" said two others and the other three puffed out their cheeks and held their stomachs as if about to puke.

Pants saw his chance and took to his heels with the unfortunate single dwarf hanging on to the end of the rope for dear life. Pants took off round the perimeter of the clearing with the dwarf in pursuit like a locked on torpedo. After 3 or 4 laps of the clearing Pants began to tire and slow and the unfortunate dwarf, very tenaciously to his credit, thought Pants, remained clamped to the rope. The other dwarves began to laugh and cheer at the unfolding scene and Pants thought he sensed a shift in the mood of the group so he slowed to a standing stop and the torpedo stood up to massive applause from his colleagues. Perhaps these little guys were friendly sorts after all, thought Pants. Pants was wrong.

"Grab 'im!" shouted one and simultaneously all seven dwarves leapt on Pants and brought him down. They trussed him up like the Christmas turkey. He wasn't getting away this time.

"Sorry old son but we have to take you to see the boss," said the torpedo. "I'm Snotty by the way."

Pants was not sorry that he had covered the little guy in his snot and considered the treatment he was receiving from the dwarves to be much worse but he nodded his agreement to the torpedo, he was very snotty.

"No, that's my name, Snotty," and then he introduced the other six as Lazy, Smiler, Speccy, Psycho, Dippy and Punchy.

Snotty told Pants not to worry as everything would be fine then they bundled him into the wheelbarrow and wheeled him from the clearing. They all took turns pushing the laden wheelbarrow along the forest track and in no time at all, it seemed, they arrived at a small hut, very well hidden in the thick undergrowth of the forest. They all lifted Pants in to the hut and laid him on a blanket placed in the corner.

"Best let the boss know then," said Snotty surveying the scene with his hands on his hips and Speccy, or Pants assumed he was Speccy as he was the one wearing glasses, pulled a large lever on the wall.

In the servants quarters of Endersleigh Hall there was a loud 'TING' as the bell rung and the adjacent indicator arm moved to the horizontal position.

Withers and Hock were about to take their afternoon tea when the signal from the forest hut was activated. Withers rolled his eyes and let out a low moan watched by Hock who immediately copied him. Withers got to his feet, picked up the two cups and poured the tea into the sink.

His Lordship was playing croquet on the lawn alone when the two Butlers approached.

"Ahem!" said Withers. "Sorry to trouble you Your Lordship but we have a code 'F' in sector 7."

"You've got a what, Withers?"

"A Code 'F' in sector 7, Sir."

"A code what - in sector who? You're not making any sense man! What the Dickens are you talking about?"

"A code 'F' Sir."

"A code 'F'?"

"Yes Sir. A code…..'F'", said Withers with a very exaggerated wink.

"What the devil have you been drinking Withers? Will you please talk in plain Bloody English man. Out with it you imbecile. What are you saying?"

"It's the dwarves Sir in Sector…… the forest hut Sir. They have signalled for our immediate attention."

His Lordship spun round to face Withers and quickly silenced him "Good Heavens man! Keep your damned voice down, do you want the whole bally world to know about it!" His Lordship looked around furtively to see if anyone was within earshot. Withers rolled his eyes with a very defeated look about him and Hock observed and copied.

"Where do you get these ridiculous notions from Withers. Code F! Sector 7! Huh. Sounds like something from a damned James Bond film. Who the devil came up with that?"

"You did Sir."

"I did? I don't remember that." His Lordship tried to remember. "Well, what are codes A, B, C, D and E then?"

"You didn't tell us that Sir only a code 'F' which is the code for 'Trouble at the mine' Sir."

"And where are sectors 1 to 6 then?"

"Only sector 7 Sir."

"All seems a little pointless really doesn't it?"

"Yes Sir."

"Right, better get going then. Sector 7 it is."

His Lordship, closely followed by Withers and Hock trotting behind, headed up the old forestry road towards the tree line at the back of Endersleigh Hall.

His Lordship threw open the door to the forest hut and strode in briskly shouting very loudly. "Where's Snotty? What's all this about a code F?"

"A code what?" said Snotty approaching His Lordship.

"A code F. You blithering idiot. You called for assistance! I'm a very busy man Snotty, now what is so bloody urgent that you consider it necessary to drag me from my croquet practice.....And, why are you not at work?"

Snotty pointed to the corner where Pants was bound.

His Lordship took a couple of moments to process the scene.

"Good Heavens! That's the Blinkett boy! What the devil is he doing here?" said His Lordship.

He came upon our operation while walking in the forest Your Lordship. Thought you needed to know," said Snotty.

"Did you blindfold him?"

"No."

"Well why not you cretin? Now he knows where you live! Oh for Heaven's sake! Am I surrounded by fools? You will have to keep him here. No-one must know about our operation or about you people. Put him to work in the mine."

"But Sir..."

"That is my final word, Snotty. Get on with it and get back to work." His Lordship approached Pants. "Well then young Blinkett, gone and done it now haven't you? Never mind, Mummy and Daddy will soon forget all about you. It'll be like you were never born." He had been working on his evil laugh and had pretty much perfected it, he thought. So he let rip."Wah-hah-hah- haaaaah!"

So they put Pants to work in the mine. At first Pants was a bit confused about the "operation", it wasn't immediately clear to him what was going on but over the next few days he worked it out.

At night the dwarves would walk miles into the mines, stopping occasionally to study maps and take measurements. When they reached the desired location they would somehow cause the land above to cave in, Pants wasn't yet quite sure how they did this bit. The noise from the cave-in would cause the sheep and cattle in the fields above to scatter and some would fall into the sink-hole and be killed. Pants would then be pulled forward and the cart he was chained to would be filled with the carcasses and he would be led back to a large underground room near the entrance to the mine which was filled with ovens and noisy machines all clanking and whirring away. The carcasses would be tipped into a large bin marked 'New Carcasses' and lifted individually out of the bin by large overhead claws, operated by one of the dwarves, and hung upside down on meat hooks on a moving overhead conveyor belt where they would move along the line for processing. At the other end of the conveyor belt Pants could see pies coming out and being packed into large boxes marked "Jasper De Corsey's Meaty Pies". There was an optional 'Auto' function on the pie machine but this was little used as the dwarves were quite old school and insisted on being in control of the process. This was the operation that His Lordship wanted to keep a secret from the outside world.

Once Pants had delivered the carcasses, sometimes there was more than one cartload which meant multiple journeys, he had to deliver the ladders, timber and building materials to the sinkhole site where the dwarves would repair the sinkhole and make good the surface, landscaping it back to its original state. One or two dwarves would be left up top to make good the area and under the cover of darkness, just before dawn, make their way back to a mine entrance within the forest. No-one ever knew what was going on.

Over time Pants had become aware that the dwarves were doing all this under duress. They too were actually prisoners of His Lordship but they had nowhere else to go. Remaining hidden and away from public view was very important to the dwarves. They would sometimes discuss ways of freeing themselves of His Lordships hold over them but there would always be some kind of flaw in the plan that meant it was untenable. They would talk of the riches that they believed were concealed within the mines and how they would extract them if they were free to do so.

After the sinkhole was fixed and all the carcasses delivered to the pie factory six of the dwarves would return to the hut. They would lead Pants in chains and blindfold him, so that he didn't see the route to the mine from the hut and vice versa. The seventh dwarf would remain at the factory to oversee the pie making machine making the pies. This was usually Psycho as he was regarded as the best chef among them. Pants would be chained to the wall in his corner and left to sleep through the day until the next evening when work would begin again.

One of the dwarves, Dippy, would bring food to Pants at teatime in a nosebag. Pants had never eaten from a nosebag before and found it a bit of a challenge. The bag had oats and maize in it and Dippy would lift the straps onto Pants' ears so it didn't fall off. It was quite dry and bland and not really Pants' cup of tea. He would've much preferred a Hawaiian Pizza. One night Dippy offered Pants some warm milk to go in his nosebag which he accepted. Pants then mixed the mixture as best he could by shaking his head vigorously and blowing raspberries through it making a very wet farting noise in the nosebag. It sounded horrendous but the end result was perfect porridge. Pants offered some to Dippy but he graciously declined.

Pants got to know all the dwarves fairly well as they would all take the time to come and speak to him in the evenings before they all set off for work. They would talk at length to Pants about all their adventures in the past and how they had come to be in the mines and had remained undiscovered for so long prior to their unfortunate encounter with His Lordship and his two butlers. They all empathised with Pants and assured him that they would look after him and they would not let anything bad happen to him. They were aware that Pants could not speak but that he understood everything that they were saying to him. They knew that Pants, like them, was a product of the special, magical world to which they belonged. They felt a bond and if it was in their power to do so they would dearly love to help Pants out of this predicament. Pants felt this too but feared he would remain powerless to help the dwarves from their situation.

Snotty in particular felt wracked with guilt that in his actions he had been instrumental in Pants' incarceration. He explained to Pants that in that moment he had panicked and thought that perhaps they all might be exposed if they let him continue on his way. If only he hadn't alerted Lord Endersleigh about Pants presence and merely let him pass through the forest then all this would not have happened. A simple promise of discretion from Pants would have been all they would have needed as Pants would be bound by the magical code of honour and discretion too. Pants accepted their explanations and apologies and felt no malice towards them. In fact he only felt warmth and camaraderie towards them despite his chains and forced labour. The dwarves chains were imagined but just as cumbersome as the ones which weighed Pants down.

One evening at suppertime Dippy began to tell Pants very excitedly about a strange thing that had happened to Psycho on his way back to the hut that afternoon in the forest. Apparently he had found a beautiful girl, with skin as white as snow, asleep in the forest in the same clearing where they had found Pants. No amount of shaking or slapping would wake her up. So Psycho ran to the hut and woke the others. They all rushed to the clearing, put her in the wheelbarrow and brought her back to the hut. They laid her on the bed in the back room and hoped that she would wake up before they left but she was still sleeping now and it was nearly time for the dwarves to go to work so they were going to leave her some pies and some of Pants' porridge in case she woke when they were gone.

They all ate supper and left the mysterious, beautiful girl sleeping on the bed and went to work. Pants had not yet seen the girl as he was confined to his corner and he was asleep when she had been wheel barrowed in. He was eager to see her though and hoped he would get a chance the next morning when they returned from work

When they returned the next morning Pants was chained in his corner again and all the dwarves tiptoed in to the bedroom to see if the girl was awake. She wasn't but, curiously, all the pies had been eaten and the porridge too! She certainly had an appetite this fair maiden thought Pants.

The next evening when Dippy woke Pants for his supper he excitedly filled Pants in on the latest developments. There were no developments, the girl was still asleep!

As they all walked to the mine, with Pants blindfolded, they happened upon a handsome Prince with a bushy ginger beard and black wavy hair. The Prince told the dwarves that he sought a fair maiden with skin as pure as snow that had been cursed by an evil Queen because she was so beautiful and would sleep forever unless kissed by a handsome Prince - such as he. This all seemed perfectly plausible to the dwarves and they excitedly told the Prince that they knew where this fair maiden was and they would take him there - after the nightshift. The handsome Prince said he would wait.

Now you have to remember that Pants was blindfolded. He could not see what was happening. He could not see this handsome prince. But, he heard everything very clearly and he was sure he recognised the voice, he could also smell clearly the unmistakable aroma of Ferret's Armpit. He was sure it was Able from the village.

'Fair maiden with skin as white as snow', 'Handsome Prince', 'Evil Queen'! What on earth was Able up to, and who was it in the next room playing Snow White? But more importantly, what on earth were they doing here in the forest? Pants had become quietly excited that perhaps Able was part of a plan to rescue Pants from his predicament, which lifted his spirit somewhat. He thought if he could get away from the clutches of Lord Endersleigh then ultimately he would be in a position to help the dwarves but in the short term he just wanted to see his family again, it had been so long since he had seen them all. This was uppermost in his mind.

Besides the whole personal interest angle that pants had in the arrival on the scene of this 'Handsome Prince', there was also the mind-blowingly ridiculous naivety of these dwarves! Had they not read the story of Snow White and the Seven Dwarves? Maybe not. Maybe they were very, very naïve. Maybe they just needed something to believe in.

As they walked the rest of the way to the mine, and all the dwarves chattered inanely about this amazing coincidence that had just befallen them and how 'nice' the Handsome Prince had seemed, Pants was deep in thought. What was the plan? What was going to happen in the morning after their shift when they met the Prince? Who was the sleeping girl? Was he going to have to suffer another porridge nosebag?

He could hardly wait.

Chapter 13

Skid Marks

Fanny almost collapsed with excitement when on Wednesday morning she received a postcard from Pants. He was in Leith having returned to Scotland on a cargo ship and intended to finish his travels with a walk over the Endersleigh Hills on Thursday. He would be home for teatime and requested a Hawaiian Pizza. Fanny could hardly believe that her beautiful boy was coming home and they would be one big happy family again.

Thursday teatime came and went and there was no sign of Pants however and Fanny was worried. After all the thousands of miles he had travelled surely something awful couldn't happen so close to home.

"Don't you worry my little Cream Puff," said Bobby. "I'm sure he'll get here soon."

But he didn't. Not on Thursday night, not on Friday, not on Saturday or Sunday either. By Monday Fanny was frantic with worry and called in at the police station to report a missing person to PC Caruthers.

"Now Mrs Blinkett. Let me get this right," said PC Caruthers in a very dismissive manner. "Am I to understand that you wish to file a missing person report for your pantomime horse who left home some three years ago?"

"Yes," said Fanny indignantly. "He should've been home on Thursday. He's gone missing."

"Well firstly Mrs Blinkett, the deadline of three months for filing such a report passed some 2 years and 9 months ago and secondly a 'missing person' is a 'missing PERSON' not a missing pantomime horse. Now, unless you want to be arrested for wasting police time I suggest you go home and forget about it." He picked up a massive pie from the box marked 'Jasper De Corsey's Meaty Pies' on his desk and took a big bite and with pastry spraying from his overfull mouth, the massively overweight police constable shouted, "Good day to you Mrs Blinkett".

Fanny was furious. As she left she noticed an unmarked white van at the rear of the station and a man, unknown to her, was trolleying in a massive pile of 'Jasper De Corsey's Meaty Pies' through the back door.

Fanny and Bobby decided that they should look for Pants themselves with the help of Willin as he knew the whole area for miles around like the back of his hand. With the aid of a map they worked out the route that Pants would walk from Leith Docks to Endersleigh would be directly south to the summit of Windlestraw Law, cross the moor and then take the path through Endersleigh Forest directly to Endersleigh. They would need to be very careful and avoid being seen as His Lordship had forbidden trespassing on his forestry land.

It was early morning when they headed off through the village towards the forest behind Endersleigh Hall and soon picked up the path which Willin had described. Willin had decided not to come on account of his condition.

They had been walking for some time into the dark forest when they both heard a strange noise. They stopped and listened. It was the unmistakeable sound of some people whistling. They scanned the middle distance to try to work out where the whistling was coming from and through the trees they caught sight of a line of small, colourfully dressed men walking sprightly along whistling the jaunty tune.

"Hi ho, hi ho. It's off to work we go."

Fanny and Bobby sunk to their knees to escape detection. They could see, as the column of little men passed an opening that at the back of the line shackled, chained and blindfolded was Pants!

Fanny's heart was thumping. She wanted to jump out and grab Pants and take him home but Bobby held her tight and held his finger to her lips.

They silently and stealthily followed at a safe distance and eventually observed the group enter the well concealed hut.

"Blimey!" whispered Bobby, "I can't believe what I am seeing! That was the bleeding seven dwarves and they were whistling the Hi Ho song too. What the bleedin' 'ell is goin' on? This is too mad for words!"

"Oh come on Bobby!" said Fanny. "We do have a pantomime horse for a son and you find this hard to believe! Besides, there were only six of them."

"Good point. Well made, my darlin'," said Bobby. "Let's get aat of 'ere."

The two walked back down the path well away from the hut and discussed what they had just seen and what they ought to do next. They could not understand what the dwarves could want with Pants. Why keep him a prisoner. They surely must be up to no good and they were sure that they needed to get Pants away from there as soon as possible. They thought that the best thing to do now was to return home and consult the lads and come up with a plan to spring Pants from the clutches of the 'evil' dwarves.

The six sat in a circle in Fanny's kitchen. They had collectively decided that the dwarves might respond well to something familiar to them, something of the world of fairy tales. They would play to the dwarves' weakness which was surely the Snow White story.

One of them would pretend to be Snow White asleep in the forest and ensure they were found by the dwarves and in this way gain entry to the hut as they would surely take her there. Fanny thought that this should be her but the men all insisted that it was too dangerous and anyway with Fanny's dressmaking and make-up skills anyone of them could pass for Snow White! Canny volunteered and was secretly excited by the prospect of dressing up as a woman.

Then the plan would involve introducing a handsome Prince who would furnish them with the details of the Snow White story, the evil jealous queen, the spell, the kiss …..and so on. The plan was finalised and they decided to put it in motion the very next day.

Phase 1 of the plan to spring Pants was probably the most boring phase. It involved surveillance. Bobby, Able and Canny snuck up to the pathway in the forest near the hut and hid in the bushes, where they watched the comings and goings of the dwarves over a couple of days. They had packed plenty of sandwiches but Bobby had insisted that they left the beer at home. This was a serious business and they couldn't afford any drunken mistakes. They were all kitted out in camouflage gear and were very hard to spot, even by the wildlife. They decided to split into three individual eight hour shifts and take it in turns to watch and log the movements of the dwarves.

They established that every day around dawn 6 dwarves and Pants returned to the hut and slept and the seventh dwarf returned to the hut in the afternoon. Then at dusk the six dwarves and Pants would leave, they had not yet been able to establish where they were going to as they had tried to tail them but the group seemed to just disappear into the undergrowth.

Still, phase 1 was a success. They had established a pattern and could plan accordingly.

Fanny had to do some of her best work to make Canny look like a beautiful girl with skin as white as snow. It was indeed a very tall order. The dress was easy as she already had the Snow White dress from last year's pantomime and she just had to let the waist out a bit to accommodate Canny's beer belly and a pair of heavy duty bolt cutters sewn into the lining. Canny reluctantly shaved off his beard much to the amusement of Wilney who thought it made him look like a right prat! With the addition of a very attractive wig and the masterpiece that was his face make-up, he truly was beautiful and quite convincing.

Bobby, Able and Snow White made their way, under the cover of darkness and with Snow White wearing a large hooded black cloak so as not to be detected, to the hiding place near the path and hid until the six dwarves and Pants returned from wherever they had been that night and entered the hut. They then positioned Snow White in the clearing along the path and removed her cloak. Bobby and Able returned to the hiding place and they all waited for the lone dwarf to return to the hut.

The hours passed slowly but eventually they all heard the tuneless whistling of the solitary dwarf as he approached.

102

Bobby and Able watched nervously hoping that the dwarves would fall for their ruse. It seemed to work perfectly. They watched in silence as the sole dwarf ran to get the help of the others and they soon returned to the spot with a wheel barrow to transport the beautiful young girl to their hut. As the last of the dwarves disappeared into the hut Bobby and Able high-fived each other. Phase 2 was a complete success.

....

On hearing the approaching dwarf Canny had immediately feigned sleep and adopted the persona of a beautiful unconscious girl. She managed to resist the temptation to open her eyes as the single dwarf gingerly felt for a pulse, he then began shaking her gently. The gentle shake became more vigorous and he began slapping her face with increasing force as if trying desperately to wake her. Snow White had just about taken enough of this and was about to get up and give the dwarf a right good hiding when he stopped and then sprinted away to fetch his associates. Snow White waited and watched for their return with one eye slightly open and her face red and stinging. It was all she could do not to cry out in pain as they clumsily bundled her into the wheel barrow and wheeled her to the hut and laid her on the bed in the back room. She listened to their debate on what they should do with the girl and she glowed with pride at the compliments she was getting regarding the depth of her beauty and of her 'skin as white as snow' except for the slap marks. She was even more pleased when one of the dwarves suggested that they leave some pies and porridge for her when they left for work. She was getting quite peckish. When the dwarves all left the room she managed to sneak a peek through a crack in the door and establish where they had chained the unfortunate Pants.

Snow White knew that she probably shouldn't eat the pies as she was supposed to be in a deep enchanted sleep awaiting the kiss of a handsome Prince. Perhaps, she thought, even enchanted beautiful girls might sleepwalk and eat all the pies so she saw no harm in it and scoffed the lot.

The next morning the dwarves returned and entered the bedroom. Snow White felt a little uncomfortable that they had been surprised and confused that the pies were eaten yet she remained sleeping, however they accepted that she must be really tired and really, really hungry.

That same evening Bobby and Able lay in waiting for dusk to fall and as it did Able positioned himself on the path a little way along from the hut. He made a very handsome 'Handsome Prince'. Again Fanny had excelled. She already had the costume and only had to trim his beard to a very neat little goatee and a minor touch-up job with the make-up.

When the dwarves arrived he delivered his lines perfectly and was satisfied that the little men were taken in completely by his very unlikely, and very bogus, story. Fanny would have been so proud. After their exchange, the dwarves and Pants continued on their way and disappeared into the undergrowth. Able sprinted back to Bobby's hiding place, buoyed with success and they celebrated the completion of phase 3 with another high-five. They made their way down the hill to retrieve the campervan.

....

Able, the Handsome Prince, waited on the path, roughly where the group had previously vanished, and at dawn they appeared again and were relieved to see that the Handsome Prince was still waiting for them apparently very eager to free the beautiful girl, Snow White, from the wretched spell of the Evil Queen. They all chattered away manically, asking all sorts of questions of the Prince having all completely bought in to the fake story. Where was his kingdom? What was it like? Was he going to marry Snow White? Could they come to the wedding?....

Soon they reached the hut and the dwarves proudly opened the door to the bedroom to present the beautiful Snow White on the bed asleep. Simultaneously, all the dwarves turned to gauge the Handsome Princes reaction to her undeniable beauty.

Able could not deny that Fanny had done some sterling work on Canny to transform him to the sleeping beauty, now recumbent on the bed, but Snow White after two days without a shave now had substantial beard growth and his beautiful gown was spattered with meaty pie gravy and porridge stains. He wouldn't have been Able's first choice of people to kiss even from the motley selection in this room.

Nevertheless he had a job to do.

He went down on one knee at the side of the bed and delivered his line.

"Behold the beautiful maiden with skin as white as snow. Never before have I seen such beauty and although it is indeed my duty to kiss those rosy red lips it will also be my honour and sweet joy to release this beauteous maiden from the wicked spell cast upon her by the Evil Queen." He thought he detected a choked snigger from Snow White as he leaned across and gingerly kissed her on the lips, the stench of Jasper De Corsey's Meaty Pies on her breath as she exuded a muffled belch.

The dwarves all wept with joy at the scene as Snow White sat up in bed and stared longingly in to the eyes of the, rather queasy looking, Handsome Prince.

Alas, the ambience of the romantic scene was shattered by an ear piercing and very convincing, girly scream from Snow White as she pointed a shaky finger at a face peering in the window.

The dwarves all swung round to behold the unmistakeable form of an Evil Queen gazing hatefully in through the window at the scene within.

"The Evil Queen!" they all gasped in horror simultaneously.

The Evil Queen was in fact Wilney, whom again, Fanny had done a fantastic job on. He wore a stunning black high collared cloak and evil queen style black head piece. He pulled off a performance well worthy of an Oscar for his look of hate filled horror while backing away from the window.

All the dwarves, en masse, decided to give chase to the Evil Queen, picking up weapons, implements and kitchen utensils on the hoof. They were completely invested in the drama and desperation of the situation and had swallowed - hook, line and sinker - the bogus storyline. They gave chase at a reasonable pace but they had little chance of catching the sprinting Evil Queen in full flight.

As the dwarves gave chase the Handsome Prince thrust his hand, very ungentlemanly, into Snow White's undergarments and removed the bolt cutters from her drawers. They then rushed through the door to Pants in the corner, still chained to the wall. He had been listening intently to the unfolding story and had been very impressed by the acting ability and the courage of his saviours. 'Definite pantomime possibles, this lot', he had thought to himself. They cut off his chains and waited for their ride.

The Evil Queen, in full flight, launched herself into the semi-concealed VW Campervan and Bobby, at the wheel, slammed her into gear and took off at speed, wheel-spinning back up the hill past the bewildered dwarves who turned and began to give chase in the other direction still yelling and waving their weapons in rage, determined to administer justice to the, surprisingly sprightly, Evil Queen.

Bobby skidded to a halt outside the door of the hut as Snow White, the Handsome Prince and the pantomime horse all made a dive for the back seat of the campervan through the open door.

The bouncing campervan sped down the hill away from the hut, and the dwarves, now totally confused, stood scratching their heads and wondered.

"Why on earth would the Handsome Prince and Snow White accept a lift from the Evil Queen and what would they want with a pantomime horse."

Chapter 14

Knickers!

Fanny was sick with worry that morning waiting for the boys to return from their 'daredevil' raid on the evil dwarves' lair. What if something should go wrong with the plan, she had thought, they may have all been caught and in chains by now. Then what would she do? Perhaps gather together all the ladies of the village and go after the dwarves or report more missing persons to PC Caruthers! A lot of good that would do. Besides, she was very suspicious that something fishy was going on with him. She had a few unanswered questions like: Where had all the pies at the police station come from? And. Who was Jasper De Corsey? Where had she heard that name before? She knew she had read or heard of him somewhere. Then she remembered. It was in the glossy magazine that Bobby had brought home from work, when they were in Bexleyheath, with the picture of Scotland in it. After a brief search in her poorly stocked magazine rack she found it. She opened the magazine at the centrefold and looked at the grand picture of Scotland with the lochs and the mountains and the highland cows. She turned the page and there it was. 'Jasper De Corsey, Laldey's Supermarket magnate opens 33 new stores country wide'. She read on. 'Nephew of the late Lord Rupert Campbell Endersleigh of the Endersleigh Estate, a self made millionaire.....'

Well that is very curious, thought Fanny. Why would the local constable be receiving gifts from His Lordships cousin? She was just mulling over this conundrum when she heard the familiar sound of campervan skidding to a halt outside the house. She ran from the kitchen, out the front door and to the gate just as Pants leapt from the back seat of the van.

"Oh my little darling Pants. Thank goodness you are home," she sobbed as she hugged him tightly. I hope those nasty little dwarves didn't hurt you. Are you alright my little button?"

Pants nodded. He was so happy to be home and so relieved to see Fanny again. He was also keen to see Zoey, Mickey and Tallulah and looked expectantly past Fanny towards the house hoping to see them come running.

"The children are at school Pants my dear. I didn't tell them we were expecting you. I wanted it to be a surprise. And it will be. Just you wait till they get home."

Bobby, the Handsome Prince, Snow White and the Evil Queen all stood proudly by the campervan, silently observing the touching reunion of mother and child. Snow White wiped a tear from her eye – Canny was a bit of a softy and a sucker for weepy moment in a movie.

"Well, come on inside everybody, I've got a very special breakfast for you all. You must be famished. You can tell me all about it."

Fanny had prepared Pants favourite for breakfast. Hawaiian Pizza which they all enjoyed tremendously and put away double quick.

Bobby, Able, Canny and Wilney began to relate, at length, to Fanny the story of their adventure and Pants listened intently too. Canny told of how he, as Snow White had lay on the bed in the back room and had only meaty pies and 'god-awful' porridge to eat. Pants smiled remembering his porridge making prowess.

Able went on to tell everyone about his encounters with the 'nasty little dwarves' and Pants became a little agitated and annoyed, shook his head and jumped up and down on the spot. Pants understood that from their perspective things may have looked very different. They did not know the whole story.

"Whatever is the matter Pants?" said Fanny. "Were those nasty little men bad to you?"

Pants stood and shook his head and jumped up and down on the spot again becoming more frustrated. Oh how he wished that he could talk like a real boy and tell everyone that the dwarves were not bad. They were prisoners too!

At that precise moment there was a loud whooshing poof sound and there was a puff of smoke.

POOF!

The cloud of smoke cleared to reveal the Fairy Godmother!

Pants was a little startled and ran behind Fanny for cover, his ears pricked. Bobby and the boys were all motionless and silent as if frozen in that moment.

"Fairy Godmother!" exclaimed Fanny. "I wish you would stop doing that. You're going to give me a heart attack one of these days. Bloomin' 'eck!"

Pants looked quizzically at Fanny and then back to the Fairy Godmother.

"Oh, hello Fanny. Hello Pants. Well! Look at you – All grown up! And you have had quite an adventure I hear," said the Fairy Godmother sweetly and with a concerned look. Pants nodded. "But you're fine, aren't you dear?" He nodded again. "Fanny my dear I am so very proud of you and Bobby for what you have done for young Pants here."

Fanny didn't like the sound of where she thought this might be going.

"You're not going to take him away from me are you? Not now! Not after we just got him back," she said.

"Oh no!" said the Fairy Godmother. "Quite the contrary, I think Pants is going to be around for quite some time to come Fanny. I think that is what you want. Isn't it Pants?" Pants nodded eagerly.

"Fanny, you and Bobby have proven that you are devoted parents and I believe that you both love Pants like he was one of your own children and that is more than I could have asked of you."

"But Pants *is* one of our own," said Fanny.

"I know, I know and as a reward for your love and devotion I want you to have THIS."

The Fairy Godmother waved her wand and touched Pants on the nose.

"'Ere, what's goin' on?" said Pants. He spun round to see who had said that.

"Who said that?" he said "What the ….."

"Now Pants! Mind your language or I will take it away from you again," said the Fairy Godmother. "Now wouldn't you like to tell your Mum and Dad all about your adventures? And I believe that you also have something very important to tell them, don't you?"

Pants nodded. Fanny was speechless and overjoyed and was about to thank the Fairy Godmother when….

POOF!

As quick as she had arrived, she had gone again.

Bobby and the chaps unfroze.

Bobby was still looking concerned at Pants and said, "Well, what is it my boy. What's the matter?"

"It's not the dwarves Dad," said Pants. "It's His Lordship. 'E's got them as his prisoners. The dwarves are nice blokes really."

Bobby, Able, Canny and Wilney sat agape with eyes fixed on Pants. Had he just spoken? Were they hearing things? Bobby was the first to break the silence.

"Pants, my boy, you can talk! That's bleeding marvellous," Bobby was almost crying with joy. "And he's a bleedin' cockney! Haha! A bleedin' cockney!"

Pants indeed did have much to tell Fanny and Bobby about his adventures and experiences in the years he had been away after leaving with Nigel and Meadow, but he knew there were more pressing issues at hand.

He began to relate his story to all in the room. He told them of how the dwarves had spent years in the mines searching for the elusive riches until being discovered and enslaved by His Lordship. He told them of the illicit operation masterminded by His Lordship where the dwarves were forced to steal sheep and cattle from under the noses of the farmers of Endersleigh via the sink-holes and manufacture pies for transportation to Jasper De Corsey's supermarkets in the adjacent county. The motley crew of listeners could hardly believe what they were hearing, but now with the benefit of hindsight they were able to make sense of some of the strange goings-on in the village. The comings and goings of the lorries at all times of the day and night. The farmers' sheep and cattle disappearing as if into thin air. The pile of pies in the police station, perhaps a sweetener for the obese PC to turn a blind eye to His Lordship's shady dealings. It all seemed to make perfect sense.

They all felt a little foolish at not seeing it sooner and also bad that they had all treated the dwarves so abysmally. But what could they do.

"I think those little dwarves deserve an apology from us Bobby, as soon as possible," said Fanny.

"You're right my little Princess. But I think we need to do more than that. I think we need to help the little bleeders and put a stop to His Lordship's shenanigans once and for all."

So they all put their heads together and began to make a plan.

The next day at the crack of dawn Pants, Bobby, Able, Willin, Canny and Wilney all stood waiting on the forest path near the concealed entrance to the mine waiting for the dwarves to emerge. Able, Canny and Wilney had washed off the make-up and shed the fancy dress in favour of their more preferred attire, the tartan trews.

The dwarves appeared on the path as punctual as ever. Initially they could only see the five large men on the path and all let out terrified screams and were about to turn tail and run when Pants stepped out from behind the group and spoke.

"Guys, guys! It's me, Pants".

The dwarves stopped and stared.

"My goodness me!" said Snotty. "Pants speaks!"

The dwarves scanned the faces of the five men and Punchy recognised Bobby as the getaway driver from the previous day.

"What have you done with the girl?" said Punchy rather aggressively stepping forward to confront Bobby.

"Yeah! And the Handsome Prince?" said Dippy, staring directly at Able, seemingly unaware of even the slightest resemblance whatsoever.

"And where's the Evil Queen? Are you with her? Are you under her spell too?" said Speccy.

"No, no!" said Pants. "The girl is safe and so is the Handsome Prince. The Evil Queen has been locked up and is no longer a threat.

111

We have come back to help you guys. I want you to meet my family." Pants thought it better not to shatter the dwarves' illusions on the Snow White story just yet and was again shocked at their complete belief in it. Also, they had not recognised Canny as Snow White nor Able and Wilney as the Prince and Evil Queen.

There followed a prolonged period of hand-shaking and introductions and one of the dwarves ran off to fetch Psycho who was still in the factory making the next batch of pies. He switched the machine to 'AUTO', kicked off his roller skates, his preferred method of getting round the factory, and returned with his friends to join in the introductions.

Bobby then apologised to them all for the way he had behaved the previous day but assured them that he had only Pants' best interests in mind. He told them of his mistaken belief that they were evil dwarves taking advantage of a poor defenceless pantomime horse for their own selfish ends but Pants had set the record straight. They all now knew the whole story and Bobby would like to make amends but in order to fix things he was going to need their help. The dwarves agreed and they all returned to the forest hut to discuss the plan over pies and porridge.

Pants carefully picked his moment to reveal to the dwarves that the whole Snow White story had been fabricated in an elaborate ruse to spring Pants from their clutches and that these men had been dressed as the characters in their little drama.

"No way!" said Snotty, scrutinizing Canny's face from an inch away. "That is amazing! How on earth did you make someone this ugly look so pretty?"

Canny didn't know if he should be flattered or not.

It was pantomime week and it was Wednesday night. Tonight was the last dress rehearsal before the first night performance on Thursday and His Lordship, Withers and Hock were preparing to leave for the village hall.

His Lordship was not aware of the daring rescue bid made by Bobby and the boys to secure Pants' release from the clutches of the dwarves, as the dwarves had been too afraid to break the news to him. So things plodded along as normal as far as His Lordship was concerned. He was keen to get on with panto and show off his collection of new dresses and wigs.

As the limousine turned out of the drive, with the front half of the pantomime horse at the wheel, neither Withers, Hock nor His Lordship spotted the VW campervan parked in the shadows a little way up the road. Inside were Bobby, Pants, Able and Canny. They were all dressed in black. Black trousers, black sweaters, black caps, black eye masks and had their faces blacked up. Pants wore a black rug. Canny let the side down a little with his ballroom dancing flares with glittery sequins down the sides and a glittery skin tight black shirt with very full and frilly collar and cuffs. Bobby took pleasure in pointing out that they were on their way to a burglary not "Come bleedin' Dancing".

"You just said wear black, Boaby," said Canny, his voice breaking with emotion and holding back the tears.

The little engine fired into life and the little campervan chugged up the hill in darkness, to the front of Endersleigh Hall, to avoid being seen. Fanny had told them that the dress rehearsal was likely to last about one and a half hours so they were confident that they had sufficient time to successfully carry out their mission well before the return of His Lordship, Withers and Hock.

They all silently piled out of the van and began trying all the windows and doors of the huge house until Canny found an unlatched window and they all clambered in, in a not-very-cat-burglar-like fashion.

Bobby was the only one of the team who had been in Endersleigh Hall before and he knew where he wanted to be. They found themselves in the grand entrance hall and Bobby led them, with the dim light of his torch, to the parlour at the far end. They went in.

"Right," whispered Bobby loudly. "Keep your eyes peeled for jewellery boxes".

It was a large room and there were many dressing tables, tables and desks dotted all around with all His Lordship's make-up, wigs and pantomime paraphernalia scattered all around. There were also many jewellery boxes containing hundreds of jewels, rings, earrings and necklaces, many of which had belonged to the late Lady

Campbell Endersleigh, His Lordship's mother and now sadly saw use as only pantomime dame props.

They all packed all the jewellery they could find into a small bag which they had brought with them. Sadly it proved to be too small and they all began to check cupboards to see if they could find something bigger to put all the jewels in. Able checked the cupboards at the far end of the room and found a large bulging holdall and opened it.

Wow! There was more money in this bag than Able had ever seen in his life.

"Here Boaby! Come and see this," called Able.

Bobby immediately recognised the bag as the one from the races with His Lordships winnings.

"Fifty one grand Able! Yep. We'll 'ave that," said Bobby zipping up the bag.

They stuffed as much of the jewellery as they could into their pockets and stealthily returned to the van making sure, as they went, not to leave any signs of their ever having been there. They made it home just before the doors of the village hall were thrown open and His Lordship, followed by Withers and Hock, left and the Limo pulled away back through the village.

Chapter 15

Going Commando

Later that night Able trundled round the country lanes in his rickety old Massey Ferguson from farm to farm telling all the farmers of the Endersleigh Estate that the real reason they were unable to make any money had been His Lordship all along. They listened in disbelief and incredulity which quickly turned to anger and a desire for revenge. Able was able to calm them with word of the plan that was already under way and easily managed to illicit their assistance. He told them he would come for them tomorrow night and to be ready.

While Able was drumming up the support of the wronged farming community Bobby snuck, under the cover of darkness, still dressed in his cat burgling gear, into the forest with his sizeable 'swag' bag full of His Lordships diamonds over his shoulder. He met Snotty and Speccy on the path near the hut. They had their wheel barrow at hand and wheeled the bag of riches into the mine and Bobby headed home.

The dwarves divided all the jewellery into seven piles and began prising out all the diamonds, rubies and pearls from the rings, earrings and necklaces. They then took all the jewels deep into the mine and at a carefully selected location began to press the jewels into the cracks and crevices in the tunnel wall. There were many jewels so this took all the dwarves a great deal of time but in the end they were evenly spread along a fifty yard stretch of tunnel. They proudly surveyed their handy-work and all gasped when the wall sparkled as Psycho lit it up with his lantern.

The trap was set.

The next night at 5.25pm the message indicator arm in Endersleigh Hall servant's quarters rose to the horizontal with the accompanying loud 'TING' of the bell. Withers heaved a disdainful sigh and Hock copied. They decided not to trouble His Lordship as he was in the midst of his make-up and dressing ritual in preparation of the panto opening night.

Withers and Hock, already in full panto horse costume, or rather panto 'cow' costume for this year they were to be Dame Trot's milking cow Gertie in 'Jack and the Beanstalk', trotted up the forestry track at the back of Endersleigh Hall with their udder swinging wildly, to the tree line where, surprisingly, they were met by one of the dwarves. It was Lazy and he was pacing up and down in a very agitated state.

"Quickly!" he shouted. "Get His Lordship forthwith and bring him to the mine. There has been a significant find. Quickly, quickly!"

Before Withers could ask any questions Lazy had scampered off. They had never seen Lazy move so fast, ever.

The pantomime cow galloped back down the track, the water filled marigold glove that was Gerties udder exploding as it slapped Hock in the face, into Endersleigh Hall and burst into His Lordships parlour. He was just putting the finishing touches to his bright red lipstick when the door burst open giving him such a fright that his lipstick zigzagged across his face in panic stricken spasms.

"Good Heavens Withers! What the devil are you up to? Would you kindly remember to knock before entering, it really is terribly frightening you blustering about so! And look what you made me do, you great twerp!"

"Forgive me mi'Lord but we have just been informed of a significant find in the mine. The dwarves seem very excited indeed."

"Good Lord! You mean a 'Code E'? Well, well, well. I wonder what that could be?"

Withers looked quizzically at His Lordship, he didn't think there was a code for 'significant find'. There wasn't. His Lordship had made it up to look professional.

"I don't know mi'Lord. We do have a little time before Panto starts. We could go and see."

"It won't matter if we are late Withers! What are they going to do? Start without us? Ha! I think not. Let them wait for us to conclude our business."

His Lordship finished off his lippy, popped a small pack of tissues in his handbag which he hung over his wrist and minced off towards the door.

Withers noticed, as they were about to leave, that His Lordships green polka dot bloomers were hanging over the back of a chair.

"Your drawers mi'Lord!" he said.

"Not tonight Withers. Going Commando old chap. Going Commando!"

Withers shuddered.

The dame and the pantomime cow, her udder in tatters, arrived at the entrance to the mine a short while later. Snotty and Lazy were nervously waiting.

"Come and see your Lordship. Come and see," said Snotty. "We are rich sire. We are rich".

Bobby and Able had picked up Smiler from the edge of the forest and collected the other farmers with their tractors and tipper trailers full of rubble and boulders as agreed and were trundling along the country roads in convoy. They were heading to the sheep fields on the moor beyond the forest at the back of Endersleigh Hall. Smiler had his map and knew exactly where they needed to be, and they were going to be there in good time.

Snotty and Lazy led His Lordship, Withers and Hock deep into the mine. His Lordship had never been this far in before and was beginning to wonder how long this was going to take. After 10 minutes Snotty turned back to them and said, "Not far now," and after another 10 minutes of walking deep into the mine they reached a fork. The main tunnel continued on straight ahead but there was a narrower tunnel off to the left.

"This way," said Snotty and he turned left into the smaller tunnel. A little farther on they could see the flickering of a light round a corner and as His Lordship, Withers and Hock rounded the corner they were met by the most wondrous sight. The walls and ceiling of the tunnel ahead was sparkling with the reflected light of the torch mounted on the wall. Could it be? His Lordship closely examined the wall and carefully prised out one of the stones using a nail file from

117

his handbag. Yes, it was! This was a real diamond. He tried another. Real! And another.

"Withers, look. Real diamonds and rubies. We are indeed rich!"

The front end of the pantomime cow closely inspected the wall and also became a little excited.

None of the three of them had noticed that they were now alone in the tunnel.

All of a sudden there was a terrific sound, an almighty roar of falling rocks. Something dropped from beneath Hocks tail and then there came a second even louder earth shattering roaring noise.

"It sounds like a collapse mi'Lord", said Withers his normal calmness and poise deserting him. "I fear we may be trapped."

They retraced their steps to the junction and turned right, back the way they had come in. Sure enough, 30 yards on it seemed that the roof had caved in and the dust was starting to clear to reveal a huge pile of rubble, their path blocked. They turned round and went straight at the junction and 30 yards on, there was another blockage. They returned to the smaller tunnel only to find a dead end beyond the diamond and ruby encrusted section of tunnel. They were indeed trapped and strangely there was no sign of the dwarves. They began to call out for help but no-one heard them.

Earlier, in the field above, which the farmers had lit up with their tractors headlights Smiler was trying to locate the two repaired sink holes above the larger tunnel and a smaller repaired sink hole above the smaller, diamond encrusted, dead end tunnel. The sink-holes were difficult to locate as Smiler had done such a good job repairing them after the original collapse. The surface had been repaired by placing large wooden boards nailed together over the hole and all the rubble and soil which had fallen into the tunnel had long since been cleared away. The boards had been meticulously covered in sods and plants and blended in superbly, which is why the farmers had never found them and why Smiler was having such difficulty locating them now. After a short while, though, he had located all three sink-hole covers.

The farmers then attached chains to the farthest cover from the entrance and pulled it away to reveal an almost perfect circular hole some 100ft deep and 10 feet across. A tractor and trailer was backed up to the hole in preparation for the 'signal'.

The chain was attached to the second large cover and a trailer backed in to the edge of the hole. They waited for the 'signal'.

Once His Lordship, Withers and Hock were in the dead end, diamond encrusted tunnel Snotty and Lazy had stealthily backed away and when out of sight of the three eager treasure hunters they ran to the junction, turned left to the farther sink-hole. They looked up and were relieved to see that Smiler had successfully located and removed the cover. Snotty fired a flare from his flare gun up through the hole into the night sky above the field and then quickly legged it towards the mine entrance leaving His lordship, Withers and Hock behind.

On seeing the flare, which was the signal that Bobby and Smiler had been waiting for, Farmer Raunchiman began tipping his load of rubble into the farther hole. Farmer Singh dragged the cover from the nearer of the two large holes and Farmer Sharp tipped his load into this hole, thus trapping His Lordship and his menservants in the mother of all pincer movements!

Bobby fired the second flare into the sky above the moor.

Chapter 16

Fantastic Hot Pants

Pants and Canny had been waiting patiently in the garden of Rose Cottage, scanning the distant sky in the direction of Endersleigh Moor. On seeing the second signal, the flare, they knew that the plan had been successful and made their way over the road to the village hall where the pantomime was due to start in half an hour.

"Is it done?" asked Fanny and they both nodded and smiled as they entered the back door of the village hall. "OK then Canny, let's get to work on you!"

Fanny pushed Canny ahead of her through the door to the dressing room marked LACE, for Lord Avery Campbell Endersleigh, they went in and closed the door behind them. The rest of the Endersleigh Players were beginning to wonder where His Lordship, Withers and Hock were as Fanny had not yet mentioned anything to them in case the plan failed.

Fanny emerged from the dressing room fifteen minutes later followed by Canny in full panto dame regalia. He looked magnificent and felt fantastic! A little ripple of applause ran through the assembled cast.

"Little change of plan," beamed Fanny. The audience were now seated and restlessly waiting for the start of the pantomime. Fanny slipped through the curtain and addressed them. They fell silent.

"Ladies and gentlemen, due to some unforeseen circumstances there is a change to the cast list in your programs. Please forgive us. Dame Trot will now be played by Mr Pat Cant and Gertie the Pantomime Cow will be played by Pants Blinkett."

There was a moment's silence while the news sunk in. Then, cheers and rapturous applause erupted as the audience realised that this year's pantomime might actually be decent.

"Ladies and gentlemen, we are proud to present 'Jack and the Beanstalk'.

Farmers Raunchiman, Singh and Sharp, under the supervision of Smiler pulled the wooden covers back over the two large sink holes and made good the surface. In no time at all they were virtually undetectable. His Lordship and his two menservants continued to shout for help for a further 20 minutes but there was no-one to hear their cries for help. They gave up and quietly sat waiting for help to arrive. They felt sure that the dwarves would be busily digging at the other side of the rock fall to free them and with a bit of luck they would be out in time to carry on with that night's panto performance. How wrong they were! The dwarves knew exactly where the three men were but rather than digging frantically at the other side of the rock fall they were safely tucked up in bed.

At the village hall the 'Show' was going ahead without His Lordship, Withers and Hock. Pants and Canny were going down a storm - the audience loved them. No one missed the pompous peer and his henchman one little bit.

The next morning the Blinkett household was abuzz with talk of the previous nights events, but in particular, the huge success the pantomime had been. Fanny was beside herself with joy that Pants had, not only appeared in the panto, but that he had enjoyed it tremendously and he had been absolutely superb. Everyone thought that he was the best pantomime horse they had ever seen. Strictly speaking, of course, he wasn't a pantomime horse he was actually Gertie the Pantomime Cow complete with udders and horns and he carried off the role with consummate ease. Canny had been absolutely hilarious as Dame Trot and brought the house down with his witty one-liners and ad-libs. It certainly bode well for the future of the Endersleigh Pantomime.

In the police station word had reached PC Caruthers about the disappearance of His Lordship, Withers and Hock and he immediately filed three Missing Person Reports. He wasn't too concerned initially and thought perhaps something had come up and His Lordship had had to leave urgently on business and they would reappear soon. However, after a few phone calls he found that no-one knew anything of their whereabouts, and what was more, the limousine was still parked in the garage. He felt this warranted closer investigation.

PC Caruthers knew all about the illicit pie making operation, he had known for years, but had been willing to turn a blind eye as long as he received a steady supply of succulent, meaty pies, which he often did and hence his waistline had expanded exponentially since the first of thousands of pies had arrived in his station.

He entered the mine via the concealed entrance and waddled noisily, breathing rather heavily as he hadn't done this much exercise in quite some time, towards the pie factory entrance. He opened the door slowly to find the room in darkness but for the blinking 'AUTO' light of the pie making machine. There was not a soul in the room and the machine was silent.

PC Caruthers withdrew his torch and truncheon from his straining waistband and began to tiptoe between the arrays of machinery. Unfortunately, he didn't see the roller skate lying on the floor in front of the bin marked 'New Carcasses'. He trod on the skate and went hurtling towards the bin ending belly up in it. The machine, being in 'AUTO' mode, sensed the delivery of a new carcass and shuddered into life. The giant claw positioned itself over the bin and picked out the helpless PC, mounted him on one of the conveyor belt meat hooks and thus began the process of turning PC Caruthers into the next batch of Jasper De Corsey's succulent meaty pies. It was a grisly end indeed, even for someone as despicable as PC Caruthers.

The next day, as normal, Jasper's men arrived in their van at the loading bay at the factory exit. They thought it a little strange that there was no-one to meet them or help with the loading of the pie boxes into their van but loaded up anyway and continued on their way, dropping off a few boxes at the police station as they passed. The remaining pies were destined for the shelves of Laldey's supermarkets in the neighbouring county.

His Lordship, Withers and Hock spent a very uncomfortable night in the mine. They were a little miffed, to say the least, to discover

122

that there actually was no rescue effort underway, but instead they appeared to now be prisoners of, and at the mercy of, the dwarves. His Lordship, Withers and Hock were fed Jasper De Corsey's meaty pies and Pants' special porridge mix three times a day. Meals and newspapers were lowered through the small sinkhole cover over the diamond encrusted tunnel until they were sick of the sight of pies and porridge and pleaded with the dwarves to release them. Although the dwarves did eventually intend to let them out of their temporary prison they were keen to get assurances that they would no longer be expected to work for His Lordship now that the cover was blown on his pie empire and perhaps a little apology too.

Although Laldey's were still selling Jasper De Corsey's meaty pies, stocks were getting dangerously low and Jasper was now desperately trying to reach his cousin to find out why the supply of pies seemed to have dried up.

It wasn't long, though, before bits of PC Caruthers started showing up in Jasper's pies all over the country. One actually had his police warrant card in it, which certainly aided the police in the identification process.

Jasper was arrested and questioned over the murder of the unfortunate PC Caruthers. He naturally pleaded his innocence and implicated his cousin Avery as the likely culprit and the source of the pies.

The police issued a warrant for the arrest of His Lordship and turned up at Endersleigh Hall, with sirens blaring, to take him into custody only to find the place deserted. Believing that His Lordship had absconded and was now on the run, which in everyone's view proved his guilt beyond any doubt, they then initiated a nationwide manhunt for the unpopular peer, alerting all ports and airports.

His Lordship was horrified when his morning newspapers arrived down the shaft, along with his morning pie and his morning porridge, to find that he was now Britain's 'Most Wanted' man for the grisly murder of PC Caruthers and there was an 'ongoing nationwide manhunt for the cold blooded murdering miscreant Lord Avery Campbell Endersleigh'.

"How the bloody hell did that happen?" he whimpered.

He didn't want to go to jail. So perhaps he'd be better to remain hidden for a time, at least until the heat died down a little, he thought.

His Lordship made a deal with the dwarves that he and his loyal menservants would work for the dwarves extracting the abundant riches from the mine on the understanding that when they had enough they would escape to Ecuador where they would live out the rest of their lives as rich men. The dwarves were relatively happy with this arrangement and immediately cleared away the rubble and released the three men.

Over the next few months His Lordship, Withers and Hock toiled tirelessly at the face of the dead end diamond encrusted tunnel but strangely found no more diamonds and rubies. They, of course, were unaware that the diamonds and rubies of the original 'significant find' were actually the jewels which had been 'borrowed' from his own parlour.

The dwarves, after six months of enjoying watching the pompous peer toiling at the rock face and the panto horse pit pony in the form of Withers and Hock hauling cartload after cartload of worthless rubble from the depths of the mine, decided that, as a gesture of goodwill, they would give His Lordship, Withers and Hock all the jewels they had found so far towards their escape fund. In truth, 'all the jewels they had found so far' were actually His Lordship's anyway and the dwarves had tired of their constant moaning and bickering.

The dwarves waved goodbye and bid them farewell as they slammed shut and locked the door of the hut and danced a jig as His Lordship, Withers and Hock walked away down the hill. They were now free to return to their previous lives of digging in the mines for the real treasures which they were still convinced lay undiscovered.

His Lordship and his two accomplices had cunningly disguised themselves as a family of tourists travelling through Scotland. His Lordship, effectively in a panto dame costume, was the mother, Withers the father and Hock, their young son in shorts and a blazer but with extremely hairy legs, were hoping to make their way to Leith and stow away on a cargo ship bound for the Americas with their stash of priceless jewels. It was though, in all seriousness, their extremely unconvincing disguises that let them down badly and they were arrested shortly after their departure at the bus stop just outside Endersleigh.

After the excitement following the success of the village pantomime 'Jack and the Beanstalk' and the furore over the revelations about the dodgy dealings and heinous crimes committed by His Lordship had all died down village life began to settle back down to a more mundane pace.

Bobby continued to work at the greetings card factory and was now famous for his corny jokes. The kids, Zoey, Mickey and Tallulah continued to do well at school although Zoey had started at the big school and had to get the bus every morning to Galashiels. Able and Willin, Canny and Wilney continued to drink in the hut on the edge of the village every Friday night and raise the flag as the signal to the other folk in the village to come along and Bobby often did and they would often recount their adventures to the other chaps in the village who, secretly doubted the accuracy of most of it.

Fanny had built up a huge stockpile of panto clothes and costumes of all genres, shapes and sizes and opened up a small fancy dress hire business. She called it 'Fantastic'. This kept her very busy indeed and Pants helped her all year round and became very popular with her regular customers. Fanny kept herself busy making new costumes for the business, safe in the knowledge that they would probably be put to use in forthcoming pantomimes.

Bobby and the boys felt it was only fair that the money, the £51,000, which they had found in Endersleigh Hall during the diamond heist, should be divided between the farmers who had suffered huge losses as a result of His Lordship's skulduggery. They humbly accepted and were soon all driving round in big fancy 4x4's. They were also able to now make a living out of their farms as the mystery of vanishing livestock had been solved and resolved.

Everyone was happy. Especially Pants. This is 'almost perfect' he thought to himself.

Chapter 17

Lederhosen and Pantyliner

Following their arrest, His Lordship, Withers and Hock were each charged with the murder of the poor unfortunate PC Caruthers and detained at Her Majesty's Pleasure pending the gathering of further evidence and the ongoing, very fluid, investigation.

Although Jasper De Corsey was released and the police had made it abundantly clear that there was no evidence whatsoever to suggest that he had any involvement in the heinous homicide, the fact that the poor PC appeared in pies bearing Jaspers name had a truly devastating impact on public confidence in the Laldey's brand and they stayed away in their droves. Laldey's subsequently went into receivership and Jasper was ruined.

Fanny's fancy dress business, on the other hand, was booming and with her ever increasing stock of costumes for hire and more and more customers visiting from miles around, even coming out from the city such was her reputation, she soon needed to move into larger premises. Very fortunately for her the police station had come up for rent as the authorities had decided to review their policy on rural policing following the demise of PC Caruthers and it was decided that Endersleigh police station was not required to be manned.

Fanny, Bobby, Pants and the boys cleared out the police station and brought in all Fanny's fancy dress costumes and paraphernalia.

Bobby and Able, as a surprise for Fanny, had rigged up a new sign for the new premises to go over the old 'Police Station' sign. After finishing off the sign they hung it in place admiring it briefly before Fanny returned from her shopping trip on the bus. They covered it up with a big sheet and invited the whole village to a special unveiling. All the villagers were assembled, including old Mrs Milligan who by now had fully recovered and forgiven Fanny and Pants long ago. Fanny pulled the cord and the sheet fell away to reveal a beautiful sign illuminated with neon lights. It said:

FANNY BLINKETTS 'FANTASTIC'

Fanny was overjoyed. She did think it may have been a little over-the-top but, hey, at least she had her name in lights.

It wasn't long before panto audition time had come round again and Fanny put up a poster in the village notice board. A much nicer, neater poster than the one she had first seen all those years ago. The date for the auditions was set and Fanny had already decided that this year it had to be – "Snow White and the Seven Dwarves"

"Next!" called Fanny who was sitting in one of the two chairs set out in the village hall. Pants occupied the second.

First on was Able who recited the lines he had learned for the real Pants rescue with added gusto and dramatic poise. Next was Wilney who had dressed in leather Lederhosen and began a very painful looking dance routine which involved slapping his bottom rather more than Fanny was comfortable with. Then, Canny was up singing a very loud power ballad in a very high falsetto voice. He was apparently keen to get the panto dame role.

Zoey was now old enough to be in panto and was eager to be cast as Snow White and she truly looked beautiful in the gown she had secretly borrowed from 'Fantastic'.

Then, much to Fanny's surprise and delight, appeared on stage the beautiful Fairy Godmother, still positively glowing.

Fanny rose to her feet. "Fairy Godmother!" she said very warmly.

"I should very much like to be in your pantomime Fanny. Would that be OK?"

"We would be honoured to have you, Fairy Godmother".

"Well, I've also brought along some friends of mine!" As she spoke, on to the stage marched all the dwarves from the forest hut.

"Oh, this is just marvellous!" said Fanny "Of course, of course. You are all welcome." Fanny was beginning to think that this was indeed going to be a very special pantomime.

The Fairy Godmother and the dwarves left the stage and Fanny referred to her list of hopefuls. There was one more name on the list, a name that Fanny was not familiar with.

"Next!" called out Fanny.

No-one appeared.

"Next!" she called again. "Is there a – Panty – Liner?"

The head of a very pretty female pantomime horse appeared round the side of the curtain. She slowly and nervously padded to centre stage and said, "It's pronounced Pantelina. I'd like to audition for a part in your pantomime Mrs Blinkett," she said very sweetly.

Pants, who had been sitting with his legs crossed reading the script with a pair of reading glasses perched on his nose, hadn't seen her walk on to the stage but looked up when she spoke. He was immediately captivated and lost for words.

He watched in silence as she performed a very lovely little pantomime horse tap dance followed by an Egyptian sand dance. She was beautiful.

"Well, young Pantelina. That was just lovely and we would be delighted if you could join us in the Endersleigh Pantomime," said Fanny.

Pants rose from his seat and nervously approached the pretty Pantelina and coyly introduced himself. She smiled and reciprocated and the two began to chat for a while.

Pantelina had come from a village on the other side of the Endersleigh forest and she too had been brought up by a lovely family with strong links to the theatre. Her family had plans to introduce pantomime in their village but had not managed to get the appropriate permissions through the council as it had been blocked by the local police and a local landowner. Pants knew who that was likely to have been.

"I don't think that will be a problem anymore," said Pants. "The local policeman, PC Caruthers, met with a rather unfortunate accident in the old mines and it appears that the authorities think Lord Campbell Endersleigh may have been responsible."

"Oh, that's awful", said Pantelina.

128

"But, why don't your folks come and join us here at the Endersleigh Pantomime. We would be glad of the help."

"Well I will mention it to them. Thank you."

As they parted Pantelina said, "See you at rehearsals then Pants."

"Yeah, cool!" replied Pants. He couldn't wait.

The two young pantomime horses became very close friends over the next few months, sometimes meeting out-with panto rehearsal night to go over songs and dance routines, and as the pantomime grew closer their relationship blossomed and they fell in love. They were ideal for each other.

On the first night "Snow White and the Seven Dwarves" was a huge hit with the audience and very quickly word got round that this year's Endersleigh Pantomime was a 'must-see' event. By the Saturday night, with all the seats sold out, they decided to go to a second weekend of shows and those tickets sold like hot-cakes too! Every night was a sell-out and the audiences even came from the city to see the amazing show.

On the last night the Fairy Godmother had asked for an assistant from the audience to help mix the magic porridge mix before putting the nosebag on Pants for the magic raspberry blowing method of porridge preparation at which Pants was so adept.

Reminiscent of the scene which Fanny remembered so vividly from her own childhood, the Fairy Godmother offered the child a wish for being such a good helper, and gestured towards the 'goodies tray', which was fastened around Pantelina's neck, displaying her choice of treats.

"I want one of those," said the little girl pointing at Pantelina.

Fanny held her breath. "Oh my goodness!" she thought. "Surely not again." She exchanged a nervous glance with the Fairy Godmother.

"I want this - Curly Wurly," said the little girl finally and returned to her seat to rapturous applause.

The Fairy Godmother and Fanny held each other's gaze for some time and both smiled. Fanny had a tear in her eye. She looked away and wiped away the tear. There was a Pantomime to run.

The final scene saw Pants and Pantelina singing a very beautiful love song which ended in a very prolonged, unscripted, pantomime horse kiss.

On a glorious hot summer day Pants is standing in a large green pasture. He and Pantelina are engaged in a mutual mane grooming nuzzle. The sun is beating down on their backs. A little way off are three little baby pantomime horses frolicking and playing a game of chase. Pants' eye is caught by a horse galloping along the tree lined road adjacent to their field. He seems to be craning his neck observing the scene flickering through the passing trees, perhaps in envy, thinks Pants.

Pants and Pantelina smiled at each other.

#0064 - 171117 - C0 - 210/148/7 - PB - DID2033153